WHERE THERE'S A WITCH, THERE'S A WAY

WICKED WITCHES OF PENDLE ISLAND BOOK 11

MARA WEBB

CHAPTER 1

"Of course, it isn't all fun and games," the pilot said from the small cockpit. "The monkeys will throw coconuts at you if they're bored, and they've started throwing pineapples too."

"Pineapples?" Deacon asked in surprise.

"Oh yes," Armand the pilot said. "They pluck them out of the ground, run up a tree and launch them down. At first, I thought they were just trying to break them open, you know, but we soon realized they were specifically aiming at people. One fella had to get his head stitched! Those coconuts can do some damage!"

Deacon and I were on a small light aircraft, flying from Hawaii's mainland to an even smaller island called *Mokupuni Daimana*, or 'Diamond Island' as it was known in English. The smaller island was a twenty-minute flight from the Hawaiian mainland, which we had reached after several hours on board a commercial airliner.

Our pilot was a leather-skinned man named Armand, who was wearing khaki shorts and a shirt, only buttoned half-way up, the sleeves rolled up to his forearms. Originally, he hailed from Australia, and most of the flight so far Armand had been very talkative, delighted to tell us what a jewel *Mokupuni Daimana* actually was. He was somewhere around the mid-forties, but his animated spirit and friendly banter made him seem much younger.

"And what area do these monkeys operate in?" I asked. "Just so we know to avoid it." I looked at Deacon and he smiled back, a slightly nervous expression in his eye. We'd come here to get married, if we could avoid concussion-via-monkey in the meantime that would be great.

"Oh, don't worry about the monkeys, we sorted them out," Armand said, lifting one hand off the controls and making the shape of a gun. He burst out in laughter and looked back at us to see our mutual disturbance. "Nah, I'm just kidding, we're not allowed to touch the monkeys, and I'm not the type that would, even if we could! We just moved the patio area slightly away from their trees, and we've had no problems since then." His smile faded and he glanced back again to meet my eye. "Seriously though, stay away from the trees at the bottom of that patio area. Those monkeys have got a mean streak in them."

"Duly noted," I said. I turned and looked at Deacon. "Murderous monkeys aside, it sounds like Gloria has picked a delightful location for our wedding." Gloria was our wedding planner, and we'd given her run of the mill to plan whatever she wanted—we both wanted a surprise.

Eight hours ago, she'd turned up on our doorstep and announced that we were getting married in Hawaii, a last-minute surprise affair, of which our friends and family had secretly been invited to. I had to admit I was excited about the whole thing—both Deacon and I were— and by all accounts the island did sound lovely.

"Why's it called Diamond Island?" Deacon asked Armand. "Some sort of historical mining?"

"Oh no," Armand answered with a dubious laugh. "The simple answer is that the island is shaped like a diamond from above, you'll see it now, see?" Armand pointed out the cockpit window and Deacon and I both leaned forward to peer out at the view.

Beneath us we saw the Pacific Ocean shining underneath the afternoon sun, a glittering carpet of shimmering topaz that stretched out as far as the eye could see. Amid that ocean there was a small green island in the perfect shape of a diamond. Glorious white beaches bordered the island on all sides, and a tall and regal looking hotel stood at the island center. From up here the hotel looked miniscule but peering at the leaflet in my hands I could see nothing was further from the truth. The *Blanco Daimana* was a 'six-story Hawaiian palace with over three-hundred luxury suites for all occasions.'

"Crikey, what a beauty," Deacon remarked. "Gloria sure picked a good place."

"Oh, that she did!" Armand said heartily from the front. "I've been working across various parts of Hawaii for the better part of two decades now, and none is as beautiful as Diamond Island, I can tell you that for free. The best part of all is that the Blanco Daimana is one-hundred percent family owned. No massive conglomerate, no huge faceless business. Victor Roberts is the owner, and a great man he is too! He personally likes to welcome all guests to the island! I'll have to wind the chatter up now; I'm going to start bringing her down. Enjoy the sights and hold on tight, in ten minutes you'll be off this plane and your vacation begins!"

* * *

"ALOHA, aloha! My name is Mabel, welcome to Mokupuni Daimana!" Deacon and I walked over to the welcome party, which included two young Hawaiian men and a portly strawberry-blonde woman in a teal dress-suit and heels. We greeted the welcoming party, and each received a garland.

"How was your flight?" Mabel asked. "Hopefully Armand didn't talk your ear off too much?"

"Just a little bit," I said, Deacon and I both glancing at one another and laughing. "The island looks lovely; we're very much looking forward to our stay."

"And we're looking forward to having you!" Mabel said graciously. "Allow me to welcome you on behalf of everyone here on Mokupuni Daimana. I am the hotel manager, and Mr. Roberts' longest-serving member of staff. If there's anything you need then don't hesitate to get in touch, we're here for you at all hours. Now if you could follow me, I'll show you to the reception and we can get you booked in. Your luggage has just arrived."

We followed Mabel and her staff up a pretty stone path that was bordered on both sides by elegant plant beds and tall trees that moved lazily in the pleasant afternoon breeze. In the distance I could hear the gentle crashing of waves against the white beaches, the air sweet with the smell of sea salt. It was warm, but not intolerably so, a little humid, and in the trees beyond the hotel came a chorus of wild bird call.

The hotel foyer was grand and luxurious, decorated in a minimalistic way that played along with the Hawaiian theme. Behind the reception there was an old man with short white hair and a colorful floral shirt, squinting through glasses while reading something on a computer screen. He took one look at us, removed his glasses and met us warmly.

"Aloha, Aloha! Welcome to the Blanco Daimana, a culmination of my native Spanish, and our sweet Hawaiian—it means *White Diamond.* I am Victor Roberts, and this hotel is my life's work."

"It's beautiful," I remarked. "You've pulled out all the stops."

"What can I say? I'm an all or nothing kind of guy! You must be the Sponks party, the husband and wife to-be. I must say you have chosen a most brilliant location for your wedding, I myself got married here only a year ago, to my precious January."

"Oh my," I said in surprise. Victor seemed spritely in nature, but the guy had to nearly be pushing ninety. Of course, love had no limits, and any person of any age was entitled to happiness, but I was surprised to hear it, nonetheless. "Congratulations!" I added, throwing in a nervous laugh for good measure.

"Here she is now," Victor said with a glint in his eyes. We turned and saw a young blonde woman enter the foyer. She didn't look much older than twenty, with huge hair, huge shades, a golden swimsuit, covered by a white sarong and chiffon cardigan that was long and flowing.

I gave Deacon a silent glance and he mirrored it back. The unspoken look between us said, '*So, it's one of those marriages, huh?*'

"Victor baby I'm going to the restaurant, I'm starving. I'm not waiting any longer," January said in the manner of someone that was bored and agitated. I noticed Victor's warm and welcoming expression faltered a little, but he nodded his head.

"Of course, dear, sorry, I got caught up in things. I'll be there right away."

January was out of the foyer as quickly as she entered it. Glancing over I saw Mabel brush a crease out of her teal lapel, I was either imagining it, or she looked decidedly irritated by January's brief appearance.

"Mabel, has the luggage arrived?" Victor put to his hotel manager. Mabel snapped back to attention and a hospitable smile came over her face.

"Sure has, sir, Koa and Liam are bringing in the cart now." Almost as soon as Mabel said the words two young men with tan-skin and dark hair entered the foyer, pulling a large luggage trolley, upon which were what looked to be a dozen black cooler boxes.

Victor opened his mouth unsurely and looked at Deacon and me. "This… is your luggage?"

"Unless someone repacked it for us, then no," Deacon said. Victor came around to our side of the reception desk and scratched his head. "Open one up Koa, let's see what we have here."

One of the young men pulled a cooler from off the cart and took the lid off. Inside the cooler was packed to the brim with fish and ice. Koa, who was kneeling on the ground, looked up at Victor with a bewildered look upon his face. "It's fish, chief," he said.

"Yes, I can see that Koa, thank you," Victor said in a disheartened way. He turned to look at the other young man. "Liam, was there anything else on the van?"

"No sir, it's still parked up outside. There was just a dozen of these cooler boxes, all the same."

Very slowly Victor pivoted on his heels, both his hands pressed together in that way that hospitality people do. "I am terribly sorry, I don't know what's happened here, there must have been some sort of mix up with your luggage."

Deacon and I looked at each other in alarm. "Any idea where our stuff might be?" I asked.

"No," Victor said frankly. "But we'll look into it straightaway. The main airlines are the ones that sort out the luggage transfer, our boys just open the van doors at this end and unpack everything. I'll have someone get in touch with them immediately and see what's going on."

"Is it likely to take long?" Deacon asked. "All our clothes are in that luggage."

"I'll be honest we've never had a luggage mix up before, like I said our boys just open the doors at this end. Mabel, get in touch with the airline will you and see what happened?"

"Right away, sir," Mabel said. She marched behind the reception desk and disappeared through a staff door.

"In the meantime, we can provide spare clothes for you," Victor said as means of apology. "We have a small clothing shop on site, and I will quite happily provide you both with complimentary gift cards so you can purchase the necessary items. I'll have them sent up to your room—speaking of which, Koa, can you escort the Sponks to their room?"

"Yes sir," Koa said and nodded his head.

"Very sorry once again about the mix up," Victor repeated. "This is most uncharacteristic, but hopefully we will remedy the issue in due time."

"Don't even sweat it," I said. I mean I was curious where our things had gotten to, but right now I just wanted to sit back and relax with Deacon. "I'm sure it will turn up in no time, and if it doesn't, it's always warm enough to walk around naked!"

Victor let out a surprised laugh. "Oh, very good! Yes, well—I'll let you both settle in. Dinner is from six in the main courtyard, and there are pamphlets in your room with all the other information you might need."

With that we left the foyer, following 'Koa' to a silver elevator in an adjacent corridor. We stepped inside the elevator, the doors closed, and Koa pressed the button for our floor.

"Sorry about that," he said with a light chuckle. "Can't say we've ever had a luggage mix up before."

"Like Chelsea said, don't worry about it," Deacon repeated. "I'm sure it's just a temporary glitch."

Koa nodded. "But eh, if you want some fish, you know where to look," he said with a gentle laugh.

"You'll be the first person I call," I joked back. "How long have you worked here?"

"Oh, just over a year now," he answered. "I finished high school not so long ago, now I'm just figuring things out."

"Well, it's a pretty nice place to figure things out," Deacon said.

"That it is, Mr. Roberts is a very generous man," Koa said. "Congratulations on your engagement by the way. It's always great to see a wedding party here. I'll be honored to perform at your ceremony."

"Perform?" I asked.

"Yes," he nodded. "I play traditional Hawaiian music on ukulele, a treat for all the guests. I did the same even at Mr. Roberts' wedding."

"About that," I asked as the elevator doors dinged open. "His wife, Mrs. Roberts, she seems a little…"

"Young?" Koa asked with a knowing laugh. "Yeah, you're telling me. She's only two years older than me! Got her claws into Mr. Roberts not long after his wife died. Stirred up a lot of controversy around here, let me tell you!"

"People dislike the pairing?" Deacon asked as we followed Koa down the corridor. He stopped at door '543' and took out a key card.

"Oh, there's been a little displeasure about it, that's for sure. If you ask me, it's obvious why *she's* married the wealthy old white guy. Mr. Roberts himself however seems pretty convinced it's the real deal. A lot of the staff here care about the old man, I guess they don't want to see him taken advantage of, I think—" Koa paused and caught himself. "Sorry, I shouldn't be talking about this stuff with the guests, my mouth has a way of running away from me. This is *your* vacation, time to relax!"

Koa opened the door, revealing a sprawling luxurious hotel suite that looked like something from a dream. Deacon and I both walked through the open door, like floating cartoon dogs following the scent of meat.

"Behold the *Lumi Momi*," Koa said proudly. "The jewel of the Blanco Diamana. We have several honeymoon suites here and this one is the largest by far, it even has its own pool on the veranda. I apologize once again about the luggage, but rest assured nothing can stop you from relaxing now! I'll let you both settle in, if you need anything then just call."

With that Koa left the room and closed the door behind him. Deacon and I both stood in disbelief for a few seconds, taking in the splendor of the gorgeous room.

"Can we afford this?" he asked me with a nervous smile.

"Hey, we gave Gloria the budget, she sorted everything out. I trust she stuck to it." Hopefully. "You heard Koa, the room is ours, and nothing can take that away now. Let's sit back and relax, maybe take a dip in our private pool!"

The vacation had begun, and I was going to sit back and enjoy myself.

For a few minutes at least.

CHAPTER 2

I had just about flopped onto the bed and let out a long breath when somebody knocked at the door. Deacon and I looked at one another unexpectedly. We'd only been alone for all of five minutes, and we were just about to get into the pool.

"Expecting someone?" he asked.

"I haven't had chance to raid the room service yet, so no," I answered. "Maybe it's the guys?"

Deacon shook his head. "No, Gloria said they're not getting in for a few days, remember?"

Although Gloria had secretly arranged for our friends and family to all be here, they wouldn't actually be arriving yet. For the first few days they were staying in a hotel on the Hawaiian mainland, and Deacon and I had a night to ourselves in the hotel on Diamond Island.

Deacon pushed himself up from off the bed and walked over to the door, as he opened it, I saw Koa, the young man that had just escorted us up here only a few minutes ago.

"Koa," Deacon said with a note of surprise. "Let me guess, you found the luggage already!"

"Um, not exactly," Koa said, a look of marked panic on his face. His eyeline flitted between mine and Deacon's. "I'm very sorry to bother you, but I've got a little troublesome news, you see I've actually checked you into the wrong room. There's another couple checking in at the same time as you, and this room is in *their* name, I grabbed the wrong keys on the way up here. Honest mistake!" he said, his hands held up in defense.

"So, this isn't our room?" I asked, sitting up on the bed. I could already see Koa hated every part of this situation.

"No, I'm sorry. I made a mistake in the commotion of the luggage mix up. I only realized as I went back downstairs to the front desk. If you'll accompany me, I'll take you to your room."

Deacon turned around and looked at me, a slightly weary expression hidden in his gaze. I shrugged back at him, nonverbally indicating that we didn't really have much other choice.

"Okay, let's hit the road… again," I said, starting to feel my enthusiasm wane a little.

We both followed Koa out of the luxurious suite and back down the corridor to the elevator, where Koa pressed a button to take us one floor lower. "So, what do you both for work?" he said and turned to regard us both.

"I'm a cop," Deacon said. "And Chelsea is a detective."

"Oh wow!" Koa said, his face lighting up with excitement. "Two law enforcement officials? I love it. Did you meet on the job?"

"I'm not *actually* a detective," I clarified. "More an amateur sleuth that has a knack for being in the wrong place at the right time."

"That is how we met," Deacon said, answering the question that I'd inadvertently neglected to do so. "We live on a little island too, just off the west coast of the states. When Chelsea first moved there, she inherited a house from her Great Aunt. Up until that point everyone thought she'd passed of natural causes, but Chelsea uncovered a murder plot."

Despite the sour context, I smiled as Deacon recounted the story. That had been the first time I'd met him, and I knew from the moment we'd met that there was something different about him.

The elevator came to a stop and the doors opened. Koa stepped out and we followed. "I love it," he said. "I'm a big fan of those murder mystery type shows. I'm afraid nothing that interesting ever happens around here. Your room is just this way, follow me."

A moment later we arrived at our room—again—and Koa opened the door and handed the card to us. The room on the other side of the door wasn't as large as the room upstairs, but it was still very nice.

"So terribly sorry for that mix up," Koa said regretfully. "I'm also sorry to note that this room doesn't have a pool, but there *is* a hot tub."

"Hey, you win some, you lose some," Deacon said. "Not a problem, don't sweat it."

"As way of apology Mr. Roberts asked that I give you two complimentary vouchers for room service. Just order a way, the first one hundred dollars is on us." With a courteous bow Koa left, closing the door behind him. This time Deacon turned to face me, and we both laughed.

"Man, we are really cleaning up on this vacation," he said. "Free clothes and free room service too? I'm hoping these guys keep messing up."

"Right?" I said, laughing also. I went over to the bed again and flopped down, feeling a little jetlagged from the flight over here. Deacon joined me, falling next to me and threading his fingers through mine. "I am a *little* disappointed about losing the pool though, my knees are killing me after the flight, and I was hoping that floating around in the water would help them feel better."

"What about we take a soak in the hot tub?" Deacon asked.

"I mean I'm definitely up for that, but I need to stretch my legs and move around a little bit I think." I sat up again and stood up from the bed, walking across the room to the window and out onto the veranda. We had a view of the ocean, the beach, and the hotel pool below us. There were quite a few guests in the pool now, and it wasn't exactly the relaxing swim I had in mind.

Deacon put his arms around me from behind and I rested my head against his chest. "You're thinking that the pool looks too busy anyway."

"Yeah, and I'm also remembering that my swimsuit is in the luggage, so I can't swim even if I want to!"

"You could always check out the gift shop with this voucher?" he suggested. "Maybe you can pick up something nice there?"

"That's… not a bad idea," I said. We went back into the bedroom and picked up the envelope that Koa had left for us. Inside there were two gift cards for $250. "Wow, Mr. Roberts isn't messing around."

"Koa *did* say he was a generous man. What do you say we head down to the shop together and pick up some things? Maybe we can grab a bite to eat together, too."

"Sounds perfect," I said. "Let's go."

* * *

THE PAIR of us headed downstairs and spent our complimentary gift cards stocking up our wardrobes until we had our luggage again. Deacon got some swimming shorts, a pack of underwear, some shorts and some shirts. I got a swimsuit too, some underwear, and a couple of items I could swap around to make several simple outfits.

After our little shopping spree, it was time for dinner, so we went to the main courtyard where Mable showed us to a table. We had an amazing meal followed by an indulgent dessert, and after that there was a short fire dancing session in the courtyard. As evening came around, we headed back to our room and melted onto the bed again, I was so full from dinner I felt like I was going to burst.

"Oh boy, I'm easily going to put on thirty pounds during this vacation," Deacon said.

"Same, but I guess I get a free ticket now that I'm eating for two. Dang it I wish my knees would stop hurting, it's really starting to tick me off now. Is that a pregnancy thing or a plane thing?"

"Maybe a little both…" Deacon yawned. Looking over I could see that his eyes were barely open. It was only just after eight, but he was practically asleep already. Flying had jetlagged him badly, but for me it had the opposite effect, I was feeling positively wired, even if my knees were still aching.

"Hey, I'm going to go and take a dip in the pool, okay?" I asked.

"That sounds great," Deacon mumbled as he started to drift off. "I'll be there in a minute."

I laughed to myself. "Yeah, sure you will big guy. Why don't get you get some much-needed sleep. I'll be back in an hour."

I left Deacon to sleep on the bed and changed into the swimsuit I had bought earlier from the hotel shop. It was an unusual little thing, a one-piece with a rather vibrant floral design. Not really my usual jam, but the little hotel shop wasn't exactly brimming with selection. Once I had the swimsuit on, I grabbed a small tote bag that our clothes had come in, a towel, the room card and headed out into the corridor.

I made my way to the elevator, the doors opened and inside I saw a gaunt looking man in a long white doctor's coat. A large pair of glasses magnified his eyes. "Floor?" he asked, stood next to the keypad.

"Oh, ground floor please, I'm going to do a bit of swimming."

The gaunt man pressed the button for the ground floor and the doors closed. He turned and looked at me. "Do I know you from somewhere?" he asked.

"I uh… sincerely doubt it," I said. Back home on Pendle Island I was something of a celebrity, but out here in the middle of Hawaii I didn't think it was likely a random stranger would recognize my face.

"No, I definitely know you from somewhere," the man persisted, a shrewd look in his eyes. I don't know what it was, but he gave off an unpleasant feeling, and perhaps it had something to do with his look. Deep set eyes, sallow skin, and a frown that pulled down at the corners of his mouth. If I had to guess he was in his mid-fifties. "Ah, I know it now," he said with a slight air of triumph. "You look like my old girlfriend."

A wave of annoyance came over me and I looked dead ahead, rolling my eyes as I prepared to address the man. "Seriously?" I said, turning my head and looking at him. "I'm here to get married, and I'm also like twenty years younger than you."

"Don't take it personally darling, I was only paying you a compliment."

"Feeding me a worn-out pickup line more like, why don't you stick to women your own age," I suggested rhetorically.

"I think we've got off on the wrong foot," the gaunt man said. "My name is Doctor Herman Klaus, America's pre-eminent toxicologist specialist." Doctor 'Herman' held his head up high as he introduced himself, delivering the words with an air of importance that I simply didn't care about.

"Well, congratulations," I said sarcastically, wondering how much longer this elevator ride would last. Looking at the digital display over the door I saw we had three floors to go—speed apparently wasn't a feature in the hotel elevators.

"Yes, I'm here on a conference actually, once a year the leading toxicologists gather, and we put our minds together. The owner of the hotel is actually an old friend of mine, Vincent Roberts, you've probably heard of him?" Again, the gaunt man spoke in a manner that suggested he thought very highly of himself, and that I should be impressed by him personally knowing Victor, the old man that owned the White Diamond hotel. "What's your name?" he asked.

"Esmerelda," I lied. "Esmerelda Gallow."

"Oh, delightful," Herman said. He smiled, but it looked more like a sneer. A shiver came over me. I don't know what it was, but I *really* didn't want to be in the elevator with this guy any longer. The doors dinged open as we reached the ground floor, and I breathed a silent prayer of relief. "Well, Esmerelda, you should check out the confer- ence on the third floor at some point, I'll be there all weekend, and it'll be quite a riot."

"I bet, *bye!*" I said as I hurried out of the elevator, leaving the creepy doctor behind. I hurried around the corner into the foyer and felt another wave of relief as I saw the doctor head in another direction.

The foyer was empty and quiet, I walked up to the reception desk and went to ring the bell for attention when I heard the sound of muffled voices from the staff room behind the reception. It sounded like someone was arguing. I glanced around quickly to make sure that

I was alone, and then I mumbled a spell under my breath to boost my hearing.

"Make things far sound like they're near, make the quiet bright and clear, dim the world, make whispers pop, let this nosey witch eavesdrop."

All of a sudden, the spell washed over me as a tide of warmth, and my hearing improved at once. There were several different spells one could perform to enhance their senses, but this one was my current favorite for listening in on things. As the spell took hold an orchestra of sound flooded my ears in what had been a relatively quiet room only moment ago. The quiet hum of air conditioning units became a load rush in my ears, and even my own breath and the rustling fabric of my swimsuit became a deafening bristle.

I focused my attention on the room beyond the reception, drowning out the other sounds that now invaded my senses. This particular little spell worked on attention alone, so whatever I directed my attention to would be the thing I heard. Looking at the door the other noises quickly faded away and then I heard more clearly the two arguing voices. It was Victor and Mabel.

"—you don't see it like we all do!" Mabel protested. "She's using you, and she's going to suck you dry until she can bury you in the ground and take everything—"

"I think I've heard enough!" Victor responded in an irritated but calm manner. "You've made your feelings very clear. Now do me a favor and pack your things up. You're out of here. You're finished. Do you understand? Have Armand take you back to the mainland when he flies out in the hour."

After that I heard the stomp of feet followed by the sound of another door slamming shut somewhere in the room beyond.

I decided against ringing the bell and was about to turn away from the reception and head off to the swimming pool when Mabel came out, her eyes pink and her breathing flustered. I ended my listening spell and stammered the first thing that came to mind.

"Um, everything okay?" I said, chuckling nervously.

"Oh, everything's fine," Mabel said. "I just got something off my chest, something that's been weighing me down for the last year. That girl will be the death of him, I—" Mabel shook her head and brushed a tear from her eye. "Never mind. How can I help you?"

I stared at her for a moment, trying to remember what it was I wanted. "Oh, yes, I was looking at the leaflets in the room and it says there is a pool in the hotel spa. Is it quieter than the main pool? Do I have to book ahead of time?"

"It's much quieter. You won't need a booking this time of night. Just head over there and enjoy your swim," Mabel said. A gracious smile framed the words, but from the argument I had just overheard it was obvious to see that she was a tide of virulent emotion, about to fall apart.

"Thank you, I'll be going then," I said as I quickly made my way from the reception.

I wasn't quite sure I could profess to understanding what was going on here at the White Diamond hotel, but I was more than sure that one thing was starting to become clear—there was trouble here in paradise.

CHAPTER 3

The next morning, I was woken by the sound of gentle ukulele music, I forced my eyes open and let out a long groan, squinting as I stared at the dim light in the room.

"Morning," Deacon said gently as he patted my arm. He was already dressed and sitting on the side of the bed next to me. Behind him I could see bright daylight filtering through the white chiffon curtains. The gentle music was coming from Deacon's phone.

"What time is it?" I groaned.

"Eleven in the morning, Hawaii time. I thought you might need a little lie-in. You looked tired."

"I *feel* tired," I said, groaning some more as I pushed myself up into a sitting position. Deacon handed me a glass of water and I took it gratefully. I could already feel that my hair was a crow's nest of epic proportions.

"Struggle with sleep?" he asked.

"Just a little. The pool helped with my knees, but when I got back to the room, I couldn't fall asleep. It seems I have the opposite of jetlag, so, insomnia I guess."

"What time did you fall asleep?"

"I don't know, the last time I looked at my watch it was past seven in the morning, so… yeah, it's not been a great night's sleep."

"Well, I slept like a baby," Deacon said cheerily. "I think we might have missed breakfast, but we can head downstairs and find something to eat if you're hungry."

"Ravenous," I said. "Say, doesn't Lizzy and Glenda's flight get in today?"

"In the hour, so we should probably get in our relaxation while we still can. Lord knows this vacation will turn up to ten when those two arrive," he chuckled.

"Give me half an hour to get ready and then we can head downstairs," I said.

"Can't you use your magic to speed things up a little?" Deacon asked.

"Oh Deacon," I laughed to myself. "Sweetie, that *is* speeding things up. Trust me, I can already feel my hair is a mess. I'm going to shower and scrub up. I'll be quick as I can, promise."

"Alright," he said, giving me a kiss on the cheek. "Just remember there's no rush. This is technically a vacation. We can go as slow as we like!"

"Very true, but I've woken up with a rumbling stomach, and if we don't get a move on I'm afraid Hangry Chelsea might rear her head." A grave expression suddenly came over Deacon's face, he was all too familiar with Hangry Chelsea.

"Yeah, on second thought get ready as fast as you can. I don't want to have to deal with Hangry Chelsea today!"

"None of us does, Deacon, dear" I said to him, patting the back of his hand.

* * *

AFTER A WHIRLWIND SHOWER I DRIED, dressed, and headed downstairs with Deacon. The hotel had a small 'brunch' menu that mostly seemed to be fruits and some leftover items from breakfast.

We sat down to a table in the eating area, a wide parasol casting warm shade against the bright mid-morning sun. A peaceful quiet swept over the hotel this morning. In the distance I could hear some guests in the pool area, and beyond that the gentle and ever-present crash of the ocean against the white sands. I took a deep breath and savored the relaxed atmosphere. I could get used to this.

"Drat," Deacon said, pulling out his phone, someone was calling him.

"What's up?" I asked.

"It's the station, back on Pendle Island. I told them only to call me if it was an emergency, so it must be an emergency. If you excuse me for a minute, I'm going to have to take this."

"No worries, babe," I said with a broad smile across my face. "Aloha! All's good!"

Deacon hurried away from the table to find somewhere quiet for his call. I picked up another piece of juicy mango and popped it into my mouth, watching the trees sway on the edge of the eating area. It came to my attention that they must be the same trees that were home to coconut-throwing monkeys, the same ones our pilot had warned us about on the way over here.

Note to self, stay away from that area.

"Enjoying the view?"

Looking over my shoulder I saw a man maybe a few years younger than me, in a floral shirt and white shorts. He was tanned, well-groomed, and looked like he took great pride in his appearance. A very expensive-looking watch shimmered on his wrist, and his designer shades and clothes were pricey too—I knew from the labels.

"Oh yes, it's beautiful," I said, indulging the stranger. "We're here for my wedding, my fiancé is just taking a call."

"Ah so you're the wedding party!" the man said warmly. "My name is Callum, Callum Roberts, my father owns the place. He mentioned there was a wedding this week."

"Chelsea, Chelsea Sponks. So, you grew up around here then? Must have been a great childhood."

"It was pretty fantastic," Callum said. "Of course, things weren't always this luxurious. Twenty years ago, the hotel wasn't here, and in its first iteration the White Diamond was nothing more than a few wooden shacks. Dad's come along way."

"I'll say," I said, looking at the palatial hotel standing behind us. "Do you work for the hotel too?"

"Me? No," Callum said and shook his head. "Don't get me wrong, I've done my time here, but right now I'm out in the world trying to make it on my own. I'm one of those dreadful types that wants to be an actor."

"Oh? That's nice. Your chance of success is always higher too if you've got family backing you."

Callum made an interesting face at that comment. "Well, they do, and they don't. Things were different before mother passed. She let me want for nothing. After she died though father took on a different attitude. He wanted me to make my own way in the world. No more handouts, no more freebies."

I raised my brows to offer some sort of compassionate surprise. "That must have been difficult."

"It was, and is, but father still lets me stay here free of charge. That's the one softness he has left. Apart from that I don't see a dime."

"Well, if it's any consolation you look like you're doing very well," I said, gesturing to the expensive watch that cost more than some cars.

"This old thing?" Callum said and laughed. "I got this for my eighteenth, back when mother was alive. In fact, the luxuries I have now are all before mother passed, I had quite a generous allowance, now I have nothing, and I'll be honest… I'm very much in need of a dime or two. I'm broke, flat broke! You should see my apartment back in LA, a dreary little thing, and I have to share with other people."

"Crikey," I said. "Sounds like you're living in the real world alright!"

"That I am!" Callum said in horror. "And I'm not sure how much I can take! I came back here to take a break for a week. I'm going to try and talk to father while I'm here, see if I can't get him to loosen up the old purse strings a bit—if I can claw him away from that harpy for a moment—" Callum paused and caught himself, realizing he had given away too much. He glanced down at his expensive watch. "Is that the time? I have to go. Be seeing you around, Chelsea Sponks."

With that Callum took off, and I smirked to myself as I watched him leave. It seemed that people around here really couldn't help keeping their feelings to themselves, especially when it came to the Victor's young wife, January Roberts.

While waiting for Deacon to return I pulled a book out of my bag and started reading. Ten minutes later he returned, with two fresh drinks for us. "Aloha," I said, smiling at him and closing my book as he sat down. "How's the emergency?"

"Oh, not an emergency at all," he said, setting my drink down. "The coffee machine in the breakroom has stopped working and Mark called me to ask for help."

"Cops without coffee?" I said through a grimace. "I'm not sure, but that *does* sound like an emergency to me," I joked.

Deacon rolled his eyes. "Oh, I'm sure it does, the only problem was the coffee machine wasn't broken at all, someone had just unplugged it, probably the cleaning guy the night before. I swear the rest of the dolts down at that station couldn't find water if they fell out of a boat. The phone is going off for the rest of the vacation, because I can only imagine what else they're going to call about."

With that ceremonious decision Deacon made a point of turning his phone off and putting in his pocket. I gave him a small round of applause in jest and picked up my fresh drink. "Well, I'm having a lovely time," I said. "I bumped into the son of the hotel owner, turns out he's struggling actor type that's been cut off and is hard up for cash."

"I see," Deacon said in interest. "Let me guess, came home to grovel for money?"

"Jackpot," I said. "He also couldn't help expressing his feelings against his new step-mother, it seems that everyone in this hotel has it out for the new Mrs. Roberts." It occurred to me then that I hadn't even told Deacon about the scene I'd overheard last night. When I came back to the room, he was already asleep, so there hadn't been chance. I recounted the story to him, including that Mable was fired.

"Sheesh," Deacon said, his brows high on his forehead. "There's an undercurrent of drama swimming through this place, huh?" Suddenly Deacon's face fell, I wondered what ever was wrong but when I turned around, I saw my Aunt Glenda and my cousin Lizzy hurrying over towards us. Glenda led the charge with her arms in the air.

"Ah! Aloha darlings!" Glenda shouted emphatically. "The Sponks women are in Hawaii now! What are you doing sitting here?! No time to *lei* about doing nothing!" Glenda pointed at the flower garland around her neck. "We've got a town to hit up, shops to see, beaches to surf!"

I stared at Glenda silently, studying her like she a was creature that had crawled out of a lagoon. Lizzy was standing next to Glenda quietly, in a broad-rimmed black hat, shades, and a black dress that covered her arms and everything else from the neck under. Black leggings and Doc Marten boots made up the rest of her look, and the entire outfit was topped off with a large black umbrella, keeping her in shade.

"Boo," she said. "I'm a vampire. This place is too hot. Can we go home now?"

"If you were actually a vampire you wouldn't be eating that," I said, motioning to the donut in her free hand.

"This is my reward to myself for putting up with the hot weather for so long," Lizzy said dryly. "If I was actually a vampire, I wouldn't have come with a hundred miles of this place. Too hot!" she reiterated.

"Well Chelsea and I are having a lovely time," Deacon said. Our spirits were both high, though not quite as high as my Aunt Glenda it seemed.

"Where's Artemis?" I asked Lizzy. I knew the small cat would be involved in the plans somehow, he had a way of worming his way into things. Lizzy momentarily held up a pendant that was underneath the collar of her dress.

"He's safe and sound in the pendant, I'll give it you later and he can bother you."

"Oh, joy of joys," I said. Don't get me wrong, I loved my sarcastic familiar, but he could be a handful sometimes.

"So, couple-to-be," Glenda said excitedly. "What've you done with your time so far? Been out on the water yet? Climbed any Hawaiian mountains?"

"The airline lost our luggage and we've done nothing but eat and relax," I said flatly.

"And Chelsea has insomnia," Deacon chipped in.

"You and me both," Lizzy said. "Jetlag always keeps me up, not that this heat is helping. Did I mention that I think it's too hot?"

"I think this is less a jetlag thing and more of a—" I caught myself at the last second, almost having dropped the *pregnancy* word in front of Lizzy and Glenda. The pair of them still didn't know, but I was past the point of keeping secrets now, I just wanted it out in the open.

A witch friend of mine told me that any good witch worth her salt would know if a friend was pregnant, but would never bring it up until told, because it was seen as bad luck. I figured they both already knew in that case, Glenda and Lizzy were competent witches, even if they were a little insane.

"More of a what?" Glenda asked with a keen glint in her eye. "Believe it or not we are listening."

I looked over at Deacon for guidance. Telling people was as much his decision as it was mine. "Should I?" I asked.

"Eh, go ahead," he said. I looked at Glenda and Lizzy.

"I'm pregnant," I said. "Just coming up on three months."

Both Lizzy and Glenda screamed, a loud sound that sounded like it was a combination of relief and excitement.

"Ah, finally!" Lizzy said, running forward and swamping me in a hug. I was still sitting in my seat, so it was awkward. It only got worse when Glenda joined in. "We've been waiting for you to tell us! We couldn't say anything because it's bad luck, but we knew, we knew!"

"Yeah, I figured you might," I said, laughing as I pushed them away. "Belladonna told me as much."

"Look what I've been carrying around!" Glenda said as she whipped something out of her bag. She held up a little onesie that said the words, 'Glenda is my favorite Aunt!'

"Yeah dude, I've totally been sitting on a pile of gold too," Lizzy said. She also pulled a onesie out of her handbag, but hers said 'Momma's Little Punk.'

"Oh wow," I said, thanking them both as I took the gifts. "I was *not* expecting a mini baby shower already."

"Are you kidding? We've been doing backflips waiting for the announcement," Glenda said. "And we totally have to get out into town and grab some baby things while we're here!"

"I'm not sure if you guys looked around, but there's not much on this island save for the hotel," Deacon said.

"Oh, sweet naïve Deacon," Glenda said with a condescending roll of her eyes. "I think *you're* the one that needs to look around. There's a road that goes around the island, and a small town on the other side!"

"Huh," I said, looking at Deacon. "I guess we must have missed that."

"What do you say?" Lizzy said. "Glenda and I can run our luggage up to our room and then we can explore the town and see what we find. There are a few shops on the high street, y'all could replenish your luggage a little more."

"Eh, it's not the worst idea in the world," Deacon said. "And it would be nice to see the sights a little too."

"What the heck," I said. "Let's go on a little Hawaiian shopping trip. Maybe walking around a bit will help me sleep later."

"If your jetlag insomnia is anything like mine cuz, then I'd guess you have two more nights of sleep woes before things start to balance out. Always takes me three nights."

"Great," I said sarcastically. "Well in that case maybe there's a drug store and I can get some sleeping tablets, because I can't take much more of this. You're all familiar with Hangry Chelsea, but she's nothing compared to her grumpy older sister, Tired Chelsea."

"Get this woman a good night sleep, pronto!" Glenda shouted dramatically.

CHAPTER 4

After enquiring at the front desk about the best way to get to the village on the other side of the island, we headed down to the bus stop outside, where a hotel shuttle picked us up after a few minutes of waiting.

"Climb aboard, climb aboard!" a large Hawaiian woman said from the driver's seat. Deacon, Lizzy, Glenda and I all climbed onto the bus, which was completely empty except for us. "Where are we heading today folks?" she said through a broad grin that spread to her eyes. "Rotterdam? New York? LA? Just kidding, there's only one stop on this bus route, and that's the village! Buckle up, buckle up!"

The four of us all took seats near the front of the bus and fell into natural conversation with the friendly driver, her name was Lono, and she was more than happy to talk with us. After a few minutes on the road, I realized she kept glancing at me in the rearview mirror.

"That's where I know you from!" she said in her warm pacific accent. "You're that mystery girl, from that little island!"

"You know about Pendle Island?" I asked in surprise.

"Are you kidding me? I've been learning about that place all week thanks to my girl Adina. Look!" Lono pressed play on the bus's radio player. Her phone was connected to it by an AUX cable, and some-one's voice came out the speakers. I recognized it straightaway as the voice of Adina Lopez, the host of Fools n' Ghouls, one of the internet's most popular true crime shows. Adina had come to visit me very recently, asking me to help solve an old cold case on Pendle Island. I did, and she turned our adventure into an episode of her popular show.

"*And I often think to myself that maybe perhaps real life is like a burrito,*" the recording of Adina's voice continued, "*If you try and shove too much in all at once, things will start to come apart at the seams. Is that what happened with Dec King?*"

Lono hit the pause button and turned around for a second to beam at me. "I'm a premium subscriber, so I get access to Adina's photos from various cases! I knew I'd seen you somewhere! Ooh, I'll have to tell Sonny you're here on the island. He'd love to speak to you!"

"Sonny?" I asked.

"Sonny Saupo. He's the sheriff here on this little sleepy island. He's a mystery nut, of course, being a cop and all. Sonny's dying for a real mystery to happen like that here, I keep telling him not to hold his breath!"

A few minutes later the jungle on either side of the road receded, and the small village came into view. Diamond Island Village was an idyllic looking place, not much more than four blocks across on each side, with colorful little shops and wooden houses making up the bulk of the buildings. The bus stopped at a station outside the town square, a two-story, white-walled building with arches and red-tiles on the roof.

"Ladies and gentlemen, we have arrived at your destination," Lono announced heartily. She turned in her chair to address us. "I come around once an hour on the hour, every hour until ten at night. The village is small enough that you can find everything in five minutes from here. The beach is just that way, and if you're looking for a bite to eat, stop at the Lazy Craw, that's my sister's place. Best eating on the island. Have fun and see you folks later!"

With that we hopped off the bus, stepping into the blazing heat and humidity of the Hawaiian afternoon. We all had large hats on to try and keep the sun away, but they were doing little to combat the heat.

"Ooh, a mini-mart!" Lizzy said delightfully. "I feel like going to the frozen aisle and heading back to my normal temperature."

Glenda's attention was on a shop on the other side of the road. There was a quaint little shop under a sign that said, 'Hawaiian Wools'. "I'm going to take a raincheck on that, I want to see if they've got any Hawaiian cashmere. I could use some of that in my shop back in Pendle!"

I looked at Deacon and smiled at him. "What about you, delectable fiancé of mine? Anything caught your eye?"

Deacon smiled back and shrugged. "I'm thinking we get an ice cream, a nice cold drink and go and chill out on the beach."

"Now there's an idea I can get behind!" I said and looked at Glenda and Lizzy. "How about we all split up and meet back here in an hour's time? We can get food after that and then go back to the hotel."

With that we all parted ways, indulging our own private vacation fantasies for an hour. Deacon and I got some ice cream, a nice cold drink and took a stroll down the white sand beach before resting on sun loungers and watching the blue waves crash over the sand. We even went for a walk in the water, which was warm and very relaxing. We were about half an hour into our little relaxation session when Deacon spotted a large man running across the beach, heading in our direction.

"Uh, I think that big guy is running over to us…" Deacon said from his beach chair. I looked over and sure enough I saw a big Hawaiian guy—he had to be at least 350lbs—running across the sand and waving a hand in the air as though to get our attention. It wasn't the run of someone trying to signal emergency, but the run of someone keen to get another person's attention.

The large man finally came to a stop a few feet away from us and put his hands on his thighs as he caught his breath. He was wearing a policeman's uniform and the bright yellow metallic star catching the sun on his chest signaled that he was the sheriff.

"Aloha!" he said through a warm smile. "Sunny Saupo's the name! You must be Chelsea and Deacon, the couple-to-be! I've been looking for you everywhere!"

"Oh," I said with a note of surprise. "Did we… do something wrong?"

"Far from it!" Sunny said with a melodic laugh. He seemed like the type that was always in a good mood, with an infectious attitude that spread to others. I already found myself liking him. "I just wanted to introduce myself, I'm Sunny, Sunny Saupo, the island sheriff! My sister-in-law, Lono, said she'd dropped you off in town!"

"Ah, so the grapevine in Hawaii moves fast too," I joked.

"That it does! Not many people on Diamond Island. Only a few hundred reside here full-time, and even then, most of them work for Mr. Roberts' hotel. Lono told me you're actually here to get married, I want to say congratulations, and I also wanted to apologize."

"Apologize?" Deacon asked with a note of confusion.

"Yeah…" Sunny said slowly as he straightened up and mopped sweat from his brow. "Look, I know you folks are on vacation and all, but I was hoping you might be able to help me with something, Chelsea Sponks. Your detective skills precede you, and I'm afraid there's a little mystery here on the island that I need help with. I figured who better to ask than yourself!"

"Well, uh, that's very nice of you Sunny, but I *was* looking forward to—"

"It'd only be five minutes of your time!" Sunny said quickly. "And after that I'll leave you alone. I just wanted your opinion on something!"

I looked over at Deacon, who didn't betray any sort of emotion on his face. "Sunny the thing you have to understand is that once I get into something, I can't stop until I've figured it out, and as I'm in vacation mode, I'd rather not get into any sort of mystery at all."

"Of course, of course!" Sunny said. "I understand, I understand. It's just a real pickle is all, I mean, how does an entire freight-container vanish in broad daylight! And all those valuable ceramic bulls as well…" Sunny started to scratch his head and then turned around to leave. "Well, I'll leave you both to it!" he said and began walking away.

Sunny made it a few steps before the words waiting to burst out of my mouth did so. "Hold on a moment!" I blurted. Looking over at Deacon I just saw him shaking his head and chuckling to himself. Sunny turned back to look at me.

"Yes?"

"…Nothing," I said. "Never mind. I'm not interested." Just then Deacon stood up from his chair. "What are you doing?" I asked him.

"Come on, let's just go and have a look," he said. "I can tell it's killing you."

"Well, if you're so insistent, then I don't see the harm," I said. "Just one quick little look though. We're on vacation, remember?"

"Of course, dear, how could I possibly forget," Deacon said as he helped me up out of the chair. A delighted look spread across Sunny's face.

"You really can come and take a look?" he asked in sheer elation.

"After a pitch like that, are you kidding? How could I resist? Now what's this about a missing freight container and valuable ceramic bulls?"

"Come right this way!" Sonny said. "I swear it'll only be a moment of your time!"

Deacon and I followed Sonny back down the beach to a quadbike with a trailer attached to the back. He told us to climb in and we did, clutching onto the handholds on the trailer as Sonny took off down the beach. A few moments later we arrived at a small jetty at the back of a large restaurant called, 'The Lazy Craw'.

"Ah that's the restaurant Lono told us about," Deacon recounted. Sonny parked the quadbike.

"Yeah, that's my sister's place," Sonny said. "Lono's married to her husband."

"Seems like everyone is related around here," I said, taking Deacon's hand as he helped me off the trailer.

"We're all one big happy family on Diamond Island, Miss Sponks,"

Sonny said. "Right this way. Sonny led us a set of wooden steps that merged onto the patio behind the restaurant. A few diners were sitting outside having their lunch in the shade. Sonny said hello to a few folks and then turned to look out at the beach.

"So, where's the mystery?" I asked Sonny.

"Right there," he said pointing out to a blank spot of sand on the beach. I turned to look in the direction he was pointing and saw nothing.

"Uh…it's just sand," Deacon commented.

"It *is* just sand, and that therein itself is the mystery!" Sonny said excitedly. "You see twenty-four hours ago there was a freight container here, and inside said container were eight valuable antique ceramic bulls!"

"Antique ceramic bulls?" I repeated, testing the words slowly to make sure I'd heard him correctly. I had no idea how anything like that could be valuable to anyone.

"Yes!" Sonny repeated. "Believe it or not we have a little gallery here on the island, and the artist behind these sculptures sent them here to be put on display."

"And you regularly store valuable shipments on the beach behind the restaurant?" Deacon asked with one brow raised high on his head.

"The shipment came in yesterday, along with the delivery of food for the restaurant. It all gets unloaded right onto the sand, down at this end of the beach were the folks aren't in the water. The container was supposed to get unloaded and the bulls moved over to the gallery, but the forklift is broken, so we're waiting on a repair."

"*The* forklift?" I asked. "As in, the one and only?"

"Yes," Sonny said, nodding blankly as though that wasn't out of the ordinary. "We only have the one on the island, and it's out of order. The ceramics are in protective packaging, strapped to pallets, so we need a forklift to move them safely. It's too expensive to risk doing it any other way."

"Okay, so where's the container now?" Deacon asked.

"Well, that's the mystery, we have no idea!" Sonny said. "It was here at seven this morning, I know because I went into the Lazy Craw for a coffee and breakfast, just like I always do. I swung by again at eight because I left my notepad at the desk—I'll admit I do that more often than I should—and when I looked out at the beach the freight container was gone!"

Deacon and I stared at each for a moment.

"Okay…" I said slowly. "Well, that's a pretty big thing to disappear without anyone seeing it. The Lazy Craw, is it popular, were other people here eating at that time?"

"Oh, you bet ya!" Sonny said. "…Though everyone was eating inside. The mornings are a bit cold at the moment."

"I beg your pardon; did you say cold?" Deacon asked, looking up at the baking sun overhead.

"Yes!" Sonny said, still completely serious. "I know this Hawaiian heat seems hot to you tourists, but I needn't remind you this is our winter. It feels a bit chilly for the natives!"

I wiped sweat off my brow, wondering how this could feel chilly to anyone. "Okay, so no one saw what happened, even inside the restaurant?" I asked Sonny.

"Nope, there's not a vantage of that spot from inside the restaurant, so no one saw a thing, but here's the kicker, there *are* cameras pointing out in that direction."

"Ah," Deacon said, looking a little relaxed by that point. "Then that should clear things up right?" He looked out at the open spot of sand again. "Let's be honest here, there's only one way a freight container that big could disappear, right? It had to be taken by another boat."

"That's what I'm thinking, chief," Sonny said. "I think you should both come and take a look at the footage though, that's where things get really confusing."

Deacon and I looked at one another, and from the glint in his eye I could tell something was amusing him.

"What?" I asked him.

"Oh nothing. I'm just wondering if you still think this will be a five-minute job," he said with a chuckle.

"Hey, we've got a wedding this week, that is priority number uno. I have to be honest though, I am a little intrigued by this situation, aren't you?"

"I am, I think you're starting to have a bad effect on me. If the guys at the station could see me working on my time off… alright Sonny, let's have a look at this footage."

"Sure, right this way!"

CHAPTER 5

$\mathcal{W}$e followed Sonny inside The Lazy Caw, headed behind the bar and through to a surveillance room in the back. "Just a heads up by the way, I'd like to try and keep this quiet if possible, I don't want word of this getting out to others if it can be helped."

"Who else knew about the shipment?" Deacon asked. Sonny sat down at a chair in the empty surveillance room, which was basically an old desk with a couple of monitors stacked on top of it. A computer was connected to the setup, and Sonny typed in the password and gingerly used the mouse to find the video file he wanted.

"Nobody!" Sonny said as he squinted at the screens, something told me he wasn't a regular technology user. "Just me, a couple fellas down at the station, Johnny at the gallery, and the guys that bring in the shipments of course."

"I think we have differing definitions of the word 'nobody,'" Deacon said.

"Okay so quite a few people knew," Sonny chuckled. "But no one on this island has the means to move a container like that, let me tell you that for free! If anyone asks, I'll just tell them the container is meant to be gone. Anyway, here's the clip from this morning."

A video clip started playing on the monitor closest to us and we all watched. In the frame there was an elevated shot of the beach just beyond the patio at the back of the restaurant. Sure enough there on the sand was a large freight container. According to the timestamp in the corner of the video it was 7:45am, today's date.

"Now let me fast forward to eight in this morning," Sonny said. The footage fast-forwarded and he stopped it a few seconds before eight. "Okay here, watch carefully!"

Deacon and I leaned in close, watching as the seconds crept up to eight in the morning. When the clock changed from 7:59am to 8:00am the most bizarre thing happened—the freight container vanished.

"What in the—" I said, leaning back to look at Deacon. He was just as perplexed as I was.

"Can you rewind that?" Deacon said to Sonny.

"Sure thing!" Sonny rewound the tape and we watched it over and over again, getting him to rewind if five or six times before I was satisfied with what I was seeing. "So, what do you think?" he asked us.

"Well, I… uh," I said, scratching the back of my head as I tried to find an answer. "The footage has to have been manipulated somehow, right?"

"That's what I think, but no one around here has the means to do that," Sonny said. "And I'm the only one that's been in here this morning."

I gave Deacon a long unsure look, an expression that he mirrored back at me. "Things don't just vanish into thin air," Deacon said. "Unless…"

"Unless…" I said, cutting him off before he mentioned anything about magic in front of Sunny. The sheriff wasn't magical, and it didn't feel like many others on this island were.

"Sunny, if you don't mind Deacon and I are going to head down to the beach for a second and see if we can't get a better look at things."

"Want me to come?" he asked.

"That's okay, we'll be back in a sec. Just talking detective business, that's all," I said. Sunny gave a knowing nod and Deacon and I headed out of the restaurant and down to the beach where the freight container had vanished. The white sand was warm underfoot, and the azure waves crashed rhythmically over the rocks.

"What are you thinking?" Deacon asked as we arrived at the vacant spot on the sand. "Does this have something to do with magic?"

I stretched my fingers out in the air to feel for any trace of magic. It usually came as a faint electrical crackle, but I felt nothing. I blinked in the deliberate way that activated my witch sight—a special type of sight that made magic visible as purple lines—and I also saw nothing.

"Zip, zilch, zada," I said to Deacon. "This beach is about as magical as a stationary convention."

"Weird burn to the stationary business," Deacon said with a smirk. "So, there's only one other alternative then, someone tampered with the footage."

"Most likely, but it still doesn't explain how someone snuck up and stole a freight container without anyone seeing it. I mean even if people can't see this part of the beach from the restaurant, they'd definitely hear a freight container being loaded onto a boat."

"My thoughts exactly," Deacon said, he stared down at the empty plot of sand, puzzling the mystery himself. "Just a second, what's this?" Deacon crouched down and picked something up from the sand. "It's a matchbook for 'The Blue Lagoon' hotel, according to the address it's back on the Hawaiian mainland."

"So, whoever made this freight container disappear has something to do with that hotel," I posited, taking the strange clue off Deacon and turning it over in my hands. "Alright, well, we have to meetup with Glenda and Lizzy in a minute. Let's say goodbye to Sunny, and we can head back to the town hall."

Together we went back to the patio behind the restaurant, just as Sunny was coming outside. "Don't tell me, you've found a clue!"

"How did you guess?" Deacon asked.

"Two superstar sleuths on the hunt? It was only a matter of time before you found something that would break this mystery wide open. What did you find?" Sunny asked excitedly, we showed him the matchbook and his eyes lit up. "Ah, I know the place! It's fancy, but it's a thirty-minute boat ride from here. I could arrange transport if you'd be interested in checking out the place with me, see what we can dig up?"

"Actually, we have to go and meet some friends," I said, handing Sunny the matchbook. "I hope this goes some way in solving your mystery though. I'll admit it has my interest. Let me know how it ends!"

Sunny's face fell. "You're not, you're not solving it?!"

"We *are* on vacation, and we're getting married this week. I'm sorry Sheriff Saupo, but we've just got too much on our plates this week to be running around chasing invisible freight containers," I said with a note of regret. "Hopefully the matchbook helps you out!"

"Perhaps I could sweeten the deal?" Sunny said. "A cash reward! Local honorifics!"

"Chelsea is right," Deacon reiterated. "We can't help out right now, sorry. We have friends waiting, and a vacation to get back to. I'm sure if we ventured down this road now, we'd be out until sunset tonight chasing down clues. Any other week and we could help out, but you found us at a bad time."

"Ah… well I can't begrudge you a nice vacation! Sorry for being pushy, I'm just anxious to get to the bottom of this conundrum. But hey, perhaps if you get a spare moment, you can come back and help out with things. I'll be waiting!"

With awkward smiles Deacon and I said goodbye to Sunny and left the patio behind the restaurant, heading back into the small village, we found Glenda and Lizzy already waiting for us. Glenda had huge bags of wool under both her arms.

"Got what you were looking for?" I asked her.

"And then some! How about you lovebirds? Did you stare at the sea and whisper sweet nothings in one another's ears?" Glenda said with a wicked grin.

"We stumbled up on a mystery, believe it or not," Deacon said. Both Lizzy and Glenda rolled their eyes.

"Dead body? Missing item?" Lizzy asked.

"Freight container vanished into thin air, and no magic involved," I said. Lizzy fist-pumped and held out her hand expectedly. Glenda groaned and put five dollars in her palm.

"I guessed dead body, Lizzy guessed missing item," Glenda said, seeing the inquisitive look in my eye. "Let me guess, you lovebirds came back here to tell us to head back to the hotel. You're going snorkeling for clues or whatever."

"Nope!" I said, almost feeling proud that Glenda couldn't guess every single decision I made. "We're heading back to the hotel to enjoy our vacation with our friends and family, though I *would* like to stop by the pharmacy and get some anti-inflammatories for my knees, they're still killing me since the flight."

Both Lizzy and Glenda looked shocked. "Wow," Lizzy said, "I'm surprised you were actually able to walk away from a mystery, that has to be a first."

"Hey, I only get married once, right?" *Hopefully.* "And freight containers vanish into thin air every day, I'm sure there's a very logical reason."

"I give it a day before she's back here checking things out," Glenda wagered to Lizzy.

"Two days," Lizzy said, holding out her hand and shaking Glenda's. "You're on!"

"Can you both stop? I'm gonna run to the pharmacy really quick before the bus gets here. Looks like we have five minutes." I dashed across the road to the pharmacy, got the meds I needed, and the bus pulled up just as I arrived back at the bus stop.

Twenty minutes later we were back at the hotel. We said goodbye to Lono, and all headed up to our rooms to relax, agreeing to meet back downstairs later to get some dinner. Deacon and I chilled on the bed for a little bit watching TV. My knees felt a little better after a round of meds, but they were still aching, so I got up and decided to take a stroll to try and make them feel better.

"I'm going to take a quick stroll to try and help out my knees," I said to Deacon. "Do you want me to grab you anything while I'm out?"

"Hm… maybe one of those ice creams from the vending machines in the food area. These thirty pounds aren't going to put on themself."

"I hear that," I said, laughing as I kissed him on the forehead. A minute later I was outside the elevator door, the doors dinged open, and I saw Victor Roberts, the old man that owned the hotel.

"Ah, the bride to be!" he said warmly. "Step inside. How are you finding your stay so far? Is everything to your liking?" he asked.

"The hotel is lovely, thanks," I said to him. "We went out to the village today, it's a quaint little paradise."

"That it is," he laughed, "With a colorful cast of local characters to keep you entertained."

"Oh yes, I met a few. The sheriff even has a problem he wants help with."

Victor raised his brows in interest. "Your reputation clearly precedes you. Someone mentioned you were an amateur sleuth, very interesting line of work. Do you enjoy it?"

"Yes, I do," I said without thinking. "It feels like what I'm meant to be doing. Do you enjoy the hotel business?"

"Absolutely. This is my life's work, my calling. I know I'm getting on now, I'm an old man, but I'm greedy too. I want twenty more years. Heck, I'll take a hundred. Once you find the thing you love, it invigorates you, makes you feel young. I'm 90, Miss Sponks, but I don't feel a day over 56. Life is good, and I want more of it!"

The elevator doors dinged open, and Victor gestured for me to step out first. I did and he followed. "By the way we're still trying to get to the bottom of your luggage mix up. As soon as we have an update, I'll inform you straightaway. Have a good evening now!"

Victor turned and headed in the direction of the desk. I decided to head outside and walk around the paths that went through the hotel gardens. The sun was beginning to set, and the evening had cooled a little. A calm aura washed over the hotel grounds and then I heard angry shouting.

"Careful with that! You scuff them and it's coming out of your pay! One word and Victor will kick you to the curb in a minute!"

"Sorry Mrs. Roberts!"

Curiosity getting the better of me, I strayed from the path and went over to the bush where I heard the voices. Looking through the foliage I saw the front of the hotel on the other side. January Roberts was standing on the sidewalk, a mountain of expensive luggage surrounding her. Koa, the young man that helped us to our room yesterday, was loading her luggage into the back of a minivan.

Mr. Roberts' young wife had her arms crossed and was idly scrolling through her phone, the back of which was covered in thick plastic gemstones—hard to miss even from this distance. As Koa loaded the luggage onto the minivan, January continued to berate him for every little mistake. As far as I could see he was doing a rather standard job of things, I wasn't really sure what her problem was, but I got the sense that she was the type that liked giving people a hard time. Once he was finished loading the luggage, he opened the rear door for January, and she climbed inside, even as the door closed, I could hear her complaining about something.

"Some people are never happy," I muttered to myself, turning away from the bush and heading back to the path to resume my walk through the gardens. I actually bumped into Lizzy on the way back to the room, and she came back with me. Not long after that the four of us met for dinner downstairs, and we had quite a pleasant evening sitting in the warm Hawaiian heat.

Later Deacon and I retired to bed, and just as the night before he fell asleep almost immediately. I tried a multitude of things to get some sleep, but as the clock crept closer to midnight, I was starting to realize it just wasn't happening. I decided to head to the spa pool again for a little swim, hoping that might help me fall asleep.

I kissed Deacon on his forehead, headed out of the room and stepped inside the elevator, pressing the button to head down to the spa. The elevator instead lurched upwards. Looking over at the panel I noticed the button for the top floor was lit as well, someone must have pressed it as they got off on the ground floor—how annoying.

With no other choice I had to wait until the elevator arrived at the top floor and the doors dinged open. No one was waiting on the other side. I was just about to close the doors when I heard a scream down the corridor.

"Kokua! Kokua!" a woman's voice screamed. Stepping out of the elevator I looked down the long corridor and saw a maid backing out of a room, screaming as she did so. "Kokua, kokua! Kino, kino!"

I ran down the corridor and grabbed the panicking maid. "What's the matter?" I asked her. "Tell me what happened!"

"Haku Roberts!" she said, her trembling hand pointing at the open door. "In there, in there!"

I left the maid and headed inside the room, a rather luxurious looking suite with great views of the ocean. Glancing back through the open door I saw the maid still trembling, she pointed over to the right and I headed in that direction, my eyes settling on a door that opened into a dim bedroom.

There in the room I saw him on the bed, eyes and mouth open, one letter clutching a hand, the other hanging limp over the edge of the bed.

Victor Roberts was dead.

CHAPTER 6

It didn't take long for the maid's screaming to stir up an audience. A few seconds after I stumbled into the bedroom and saw the dead Mr. Roberts another maid ran in behind me, gasped in response and covered her mouth with her hands.

"Ua make?" she said in a questioning tone.

"Pardon me?" I asked, not understanding her native tongue.

"He's dead?" she repeated, tears brimming in her eyes. I didn't have to check a pulse to confirm as much, his eyes were open and dull, and there was no movement on his chest. I nodded my head to indicate he was.

"Yes, I'm sorry. Let's go back to the corridor," I said, taking the young girl by the shoulder and leading her out of the bedroom. "We should call the police."

Outside in the corridor a number of people were now gathered, some people were trying to console the hysterical maid I had initially heard from the elevator. A man in a bathrobe rushed towards the door as we were coming out.

"What's going on in there?" he asked. I recognized the man as Doctor Herman Klaus, the unpleasant individual I'd met in the elevator the day before.

"It's Mr. Roberts, he's dead. We should stay out here until the police arrive."

"Bully to that!" Klaus barked as he pushed his way past me. "Victor, Victor!" he called as he stormed into the room. I asked one of the people in the corridor to console the shocked maid I'd just escorted out of the bedroom and turned to follow Doctor Herman Klaus. I saw him stood still in the doorway of the dim bedroom, staring at the body of his dead friend.

"Do you believe me now? There's nothing you can do for him doctor; it looks like he's been dead for some time."

Klaus took no notice of me and rushed towards the body, crouching to try for a pulse. After a moment he looked up at me, his face grey and ashen from shock. "He *is* dead. Call the police, now!"

"That's what I was trying to do," I said through gritted teeth. "You need to go out into the corridor with the others, you're contaminating the scene."

Doctor Herman Klaus' brow knit in confusion. "What are you talking about? Contaminating the scene?" As he said that he lost his balance and nudged the bedside table, almost spilling a glass of water.

"As in stop touching stuff, you dummy," I said coldly. "Stand up and get out of the room, *now.*"

Any bystander might think I used magic to get the irritable Doctor Klaus out of the room, but I resorted to the oldest magic of all —the ire of a woman. Klaus seemed to recognize I wasn't messing around now and he stood up quickly, mumbling something about 'only trying to help' as he left the room and went back to the corridor. I followed close behind to make sure he didn't mess anything else up.

Back in the corridor a crowd was quickly building now, and it seemed that everyone sleeping on this floor was now awake due to the commotion.

"Is it true?" a man asked me. "Is he really dead?"

"Sadly, it appears so, yes," I said. A shocked reaction passed through the crowd. I looked at the young maid I had escorted out of the bedroom. "Has anyone called the police?"

"I have," a heavy-set woman in a silk kimono said from the back of the crowd. They're coming with paramedics now!"

"Paramedics aren't going to do anything," I mumbled under my breath.

Before long the police did arrive, the familiar face of Sheriff Sunny Saupo cutting his way through the corridor. "Alright folks, alright, back to your rooms now, let the professionals through." Despite the late hour and the grim context Sunny still had a warm countenance and a melodic quality to his voice, which seemed to put people at ease. Hotel staff were packed amongst the crowd, and they helped disperse the guests. As people cleared out there was just the police, the hotel staff, me, and Doctor Herman Klaus, who seemed intent on sticking around for some reason.

Sunny saw me standing by the door and made an expression of acknowledgement.

"Ah, Miss Chelsea Sponks, I thought I might see you here! Who discovered the body?"

"I'au," said the maid I had originally heard from elevator. "I was bringing him his nightly supper. I walked in and saw him there, dead on the bed. Then I started screaming, and this young woman here came running to me."

Sunny looked at me with a raised brow. "Always in the thick of it, eh Sponks? Let's take a look then." Sunny and the two police officers accompanying—a man and woman—went into the room to inspect the body. After a few moments Sunny came out again clutching a piece of paper, I recognized it as the one in Victor's hand. "Did you see this?" he asked me. "It was in Mr. Victor Roberts' hand. A suicide note?"

"Yes, I didn't want to touch anything and compromise the scene."

Sunny nodded astutely. He didn't have gloves on, but it wasn't uncommon for initial responders to handle things without gloves, they could always excuse their prints from forensics afterwards. As if reading my mind Sunny did pull out a pair of gloves and slipped them on before handling the letter any further. He unfolded it and read it out loud.

"I'm sorry, but I just can't bear to go on any longer. 3938." Sunny folded the letter and looked up. "3938?" he repeated, phrasing the question to himself.

"A code!" Herman said, an animated look in his eye. "I know, one second!" The doctor hurried off quickly to his room. Sunny looked at one of his men. "I thought we told guests to go back to their rooms."

"I tried chief," the cop answered. "He said he was a VIP, an esteemed friend of Victor Roberts."

"I know who he is, I've seen him around here plenty of times, but I don't want guests contaminating the scene."

"Already did," I said. "He checked for a pulse and nearly knocked the bedside table over." Sunny rolled his eyes. "Anyway, you seem to have a handle on things here, chief, I'll leave you to it," I said and turned to go.

"Hold on a minute now Sponks," Sunny said. "You might be a guest, but I think we can make an exception provided you have experience with this sort of thing. I know you're on your vacation, but this is right up your alley, is it not?"

"I uh…" I faltered, trying to think of any excuse to get out of there, but truthfully, I was in my element with this 'sort of thing', and with my current insomnia, going back to the hotel room and staring at the ceiling for six hours wasn't exactly a better alternative. "I'll give you a few minutes. I can't sleep at the moment anyway."

"Jetlag, eh?" Sunny said with a note of amusement. "I get it terribly too."

Herman Klaus rushed back into the corridor holding a bible. "Here!" he said excitedly. "39:38! *'The gold altar, the special olive oil used for appointing priests, the sweet-smelling incense, and the curtain that covered the entrance to the Tent!'"*

Everyone else stared at one another for an uncomfortable moment as Doctor Herman Klaus shut the bible and looked up enthusiastically.

"Is that supposed to mean something?" Sheriff Sunny asked with uncertainty.

"Why, isn't it obvious?!" Doctor Herman Klaus said. "Victor obviously left us a clue, and if you read between the lines of that note, I think he was reaching out to me, his dearest friend!"

"Verity, re-read that note," Sunny said to the female officer that was now holding the suicide note.

Verity cleared her throat and read the note. *"I'm sorry, but I just can't bear to go on any longer. 3938."*

I looked at Herman Klaus. "Either I'm missing something here, of you're suffering from a mighty case of main character syndrome."

"I'm not familiar with that ailment," the doctor said.

"It's when you think the world revolves around you. A man died and you're convinced his suicide note—which mentions no one by name—must have something to do with you," I said, wondering when Sunny would have the insufferable doctor escorted back to his room.

"Ignorance begets you," Klaus said sharply. "The clue is in the numbers. 3938. Chapter 39, Verse 38. I'm a deeply religious man, and Victor knew my favorite book of the bible is Exodus. It's a clue, but I don't know what it means! Gold altar? Special olive oil? What could it mean?!"

"It means nothing, because you're making assumptions and working backwards to make evidence fit your theory," I said.

"I'm with Miss Sponks on this one, doctor, and I'm going to have to ask you to go back to your room now," Sunny said to Herman Klaus.

"But I'm one of Victor's oldest friends!"

"And all the better reason to be out of this. You're in shock, friend. Please go to bed, we'll talk with you tomorrow if we need to." Sunny nodded at his supporting officers to escort Herman back to his room. He realized he was outnumbered and left begrudgingly.

"You!" he shouted to me as he left. "Remember the verse! Gold altar, special olive oil! It means something!"

One of the officers went into the room with Herman and closed the door, presumably keeping guard to make sure the man didn't try and insert himself into the proceedings again.

"Alright," Sunny said, "Let's take another look at the scene. Miss

Sponks, if you'd so gladly accompany me? Verity, keep guard of the door and see when Jill can come down."

"Yes, chief."

Sunny got the names of the two maids and asked them to wait in the suite before more officers arrived to help with questioning.

We headed back into the room, Sunny handing me a pair of gloves this time, and covers to go over my shoes. We stepped into the bedroom and turned on the light. For a few moments the pair of us silently assessed the scene before saying anything.

"It's very unusual," he said after a few seconds.

"What's that?" I asked.

"I knew Victor Roberts quite well, and I had no idea he was struggling with something like this. He hid it well. But how did he do it?"

I walked forward and examined the items scattered across the bedside table. There was a glass of water, reading glasses, a book, and a blank notepad with a sheet half torn out. A trashcan beside the bedside table was empty except for one thing, I pulled it out and held it in the air.

"Perhaps this?" I asked.

"What is it?" Sunny asked.

"Oxycontin," I said, reading the box. "It's a high-strength prescription painkiller. The active ingredient is morphine."

Sunny's eyes widened in surprise. "Morphine? That would almost certainly be enough to do it."

Turning over the box I saw a sticker on the other side, with the prescription details. "It says here these pills were prescribed to a Mrs. January Roberts, and this prescription was filled today."

"And the box is empty?" Sunny asked. I pulled out two empty blister packs and nodded. "So, Victor took the entire box today! Almost certainly this has to be the way he killed himself."

"Early signs indicate it's possible," I said. "Who's Jill? You asked your officer to have her come over."

"Jill's my swiss-army knife," Sunny said, smiling as his eyes moved over the scene. "Island forensics, *and* the island coroner."

"Must be a busy woman," I reasoned.

"Hardly, nothing ever happens here. The main cause of death in paradise is old age, Miss Sponks."

I set the empty box of pills on the table and walked around the bed to the windows. There were two of them, the kind that opened upwards by sliding in the frame. The one on the right was open a crack. I crouched down and considered the frame carefully.

"What is it?" Sunny asked me.

"The paint is missing from the inside of this window frame." I stood up again and looked around the room, noticing that the walls and ceiling looked slightly stained, as if they had been brushed lightly with a shade of something dark. "Is there damp in here?"

"Possibly," Sunny said. "It does get humid here, but I imagine a man like Victor Roberts would have some high-end HVAC system. Air conditioning is like gold on an island like this."

"And almost standard for a luxury hotel." I looked around the room for a vent and found one above the door. It was out of reach, so I pulled a chair from a writing desk in the corner, stood on it and pressed my fingertips against the vent. My gloves stuck to the surface momentarily as I pulled my hand away, there was some sort of tacky residue. "Interesting," I said.

"Miss Sponks, I find myself confused," Sunny said as I climbed back down again. "What avenue of thought are you running down? This is an open and shut case, is it not? Mr. Roberts has unfortunately killed himself, and it seems most likely the cause of death was an intentional morphine overdose. Why the pill box is right there, and he left a note!"

"That he did. Can you fetch that for me?" Sunny left the room and came back with the note. I compared it to the notebook and found the tear matched up. "I just find myself a little baffled."

"Baffled?" Sunny laughed in confusion. "Whatever do you mean?"

With nothing else to see I left the room and Sunny accompanied me, closing the door as he did so. "I know I didn't know the man well, but I spoke with Mr. Roberts a few times while staying here at the hotel, and he didn't strike me as the suicidal type at all."

"Ah yes, but people have a way of hiding these things, do they not? What is the saying, those that laugh the most, cry the hardest?"

"You think he was secretly suicidal?" I asked Sunny.

"If you asked me before today, I would have said no, but the unfortunate state we have found Mr. Roberts in, I think it more than certainly casts aside any question of him being suicidal or not."

"I suppose that's one way of looking at it," I said, my arms held behind my back as I walked across the suite. Both maids were sitting with police officers now, giving statements about their impressions of the scene. I turned and looked at Sunny.

"If it's not much trouble I'll need a quick statement," he said. I agreed, we both sat and I gave a quick recap of the events as they unfolded. When I was done Sunny thanked me. A short Hawaiian woman in a long black jacket came into the room, a large suitcase rolling along the floor behind her.

"Don't tell me, I've got the wrong room. This doesn't look like my suite," the woman said in a dry tone that suggested she was joking.

"Jill!" Sunny said, rising out of his chair and greeting her warmly. I also stood. Sunny introduced us both, giving equal praise to both sides for our respective skills.

"Sleuth extraordinaire, eh?" Jill said with keen interest. "How is it you sleuth types always end up on the scene before anyone else?"

I shrugged, admittedly I'd often wondered the same thing myself. "Plain bad luck, I guess." Jill laughed and looked at Sunny.

"Victor Roberts then, where is he, the bedroom?"

"Yes," Sunny said gravely. "We believe it to be suicide by morphine. There's an empty box of pills in the bin, prescribed today."

Jill grimaced, grabbed the handle of her suitcase, getting ready to pull it behind her again. "Sounds almost certainly like you found the trick, though I suppose I'm still obliged to let the science give us the final verdict. My assistant, Rodney, will be along shortly with a gurney. We'll get the body back to the lab and start running the results right away. I'll take the scene from here Sunny, thanks. I'd like your men and everyone else out of this suite. Nice meeting you, Miss Sponks."

We all filed out of Victor Roberts' suite, leaving the investigation to Sunny's swiss-army-knife, Jill. Out in the corridor Sunny instructed his men to set up temporary posts to make sure no one else interfered with the scene while Jill was working. Sunny turned to me and frowned sympathetically. "Sorry Miss Sponks, it seems you're not getting a mystery here," Sunny said apologetically. "Things look pretty straightforward, although a little surprising, as you yourself said."

"I suspect you are most likely correct," I admitted. "But I still find myself with questions."

"Such as?" Sunny probed.

"…I will leave them with myself for now. Let's see what the coroner turns up and then we can talk some more. There's still the element of the numbers at the end of the suicide note. What do they mean?"

"That remains to be determined," Sunny agreed. "But hey, there's still the case of that missing freight container we talked about earlier. I bet that could keep you busy!"

I smiled meekly. Even though the missing freight container *was* confounding, something about it didn't seem quite right to me. "Yes, well as I mentioned, I'm already occupied with another mystery—how does one relax on vacation?"

Sunny laughed. "Message received loud and clear. I'll say good-night to you Miss Sponks, or I would if you were able to get any sleep. Try warm milk and chamomile. It always helps me."

"I'll consider it, thanks sheriff."

With that I returned to the elevator, and I made my way down-stairs. I half-considered just going back to the room and trying to sleep, but my mind was much too preoccupied to sleep, and that wasn't even taking insomnia into account.

I went to the spa pool and lost myself in thought while I did laps in the water. It was quiet and serene, a nice bout of relaxation to end the day. After thirty minutes or so of laps I got out again, dried off and made my way back to the bedroom. Deacon was still sleeping soundly on the bed and didn't stir while I showered and changed. I slipped into bed beside him and cuddled up against him, my eyes beginning to lull within seconds of my head touching the pillow.

Even though my mind was racing with questions from the night's bizarre events I felt calm, as though enigma was a natural state of relaxation for me. For the most part things did look straightforward in this unusual and sad case, but certain elements didn't quite add up. One of them came to me the following day however, just after breakfast.

I knew what the numbers at the end of the letter meant.

CHAPTER 7

"Let me get this straight," Deacon said, almost laughing in disbelief as he drank coffee on our veranda. "You went out for a nightly swim, and in the process, you stumbled upon a dead body?"

"Not just any dead body! Victor Roberts, the old man that runs the hotel!" I said, sitting down to join him at the table. I'd only just woken and made my way out to talk to him.

"You're unbelievable," he said in an amused way. "I mean, you really have a gift for this stuff. You're like a magnet for dead bodies."

"You don't have to tell me."

"What's the verdict then?" Deacon asked. "How did the old man die?"

"It looks like a suicide, morphine overdose. He left a short note saying how he couldn't go on, and it had these mysterious numbers at the end."

"Uh huh," Deacon said and took a sip of his coffee.

"What's that supposed to mean?" I asked. His tone suggested he thought there was more to the story.

"Well, go on then, let's hear the rest of it. There's always a 'but' with you, especially when it comes to this sort of thing!" Deacon said with a laugh.

My mouth was open ready to argue the point, but Deacon had me. "It's just… I don't know, something felt off to me about the whole thing."

"I'm impressed, you didn't say 'but'. What was off about it?"

"I don't know, I'm probably just looking for trouble where there is none. The whole world looks like a nail when you're a hammer, you know, that sort of thing? There is one thing though, I spoke with Victor Roberts yesterday in the elevator, and he was going on about how he wanted twenty more years, how he loved every day, and all he wanted was more!"

"Huh," Deacon said, raising one brow in intrigue. "Definitely doesn't seem like something a suicidal person would say, even if they were masking."

"That's exactly what I'm thinking! But I digress, the simplest explanation is probably the most rational one, I'm going to leave it in the hands of the police and enjoy our time—" A knock came at the bedroom door, and I turned.

"Any guesses on who's knocking at the door?" Deacon said with a smirk. He got up from the table and went over to open the door. Upon opening it Glenda and Lizzy came in.

"Surprise!" Glenda said as they barged into the apartment. "We're here to cook breakfast!"

"What?" Deacon asked, watching as my aunt and cousin stormed in.

"Yeah, what?" I mirrored, standing up to head into the apartment from the balcony.

Lizzy set bags down on the counter in the apartment's kitchenette. "Glenda and I woke early this morning and went to get a head start on breakfast, but apparently they're not serving breakfast today. Apparently—Chelsea you're going to love this one—one of the staff died last night and that's disrupted the service schedule. There are police everywhere! Glenda and I took a bus into town and got supplies to make breakfast. Surprise!"

"I had a sneaking suspicion this vacation would have some sort of police element," Glenda said as she started unpacking their breakfast items onto the counters. She pulled out pans from the kitchenette cupboards, fired up the small hob and started cracking eggs. "Trouble follows us everywhere after all. We're taking bets on what happened, we tried to weasel it out of the cops in the foyer, but they're being tight-lipped. Lizzy thinks—"

"It's Victor Roberts," I said, "the old man that owns the hotel. They found him dead In his room last night, suspected morphine overdose."

Lizzy and Glenda looked at one another in bewilderment. "Of course, she knows!" Lizzy said, rolling her eyes in disbelief. I recounted the story of the night before once more to Lizzy and Glenda, who were both intrigued and also amused at me stumbling my way into another crime scene.

We talked over the unusual events as we ate at the breakfast bar in our suite. Halfway through the meal Lizzy pulled something from out of her bag and handed it to me. "Here, you take him now, he's been driving me mad."

Lizzy pushed a locket across the table, it was the magical device we'd crafted to help transport my talking familiar—Artemis. The magical locket was a way of transporting Artemis around with little trouble. The pink gemstone set into the locket was a button that could store and retrieve Artemis at a moment's notice, sucking him up and spitting him out like a ghost into a vacuum.

While in there he could also project an astral form of himself, which only Lizzy and I could see. I hadn't seen Artemis since getting here so I decided to bring him out. I pressed the button and his small black form whooshed out of the locket and appeared on the back of a chair next to the breakfast table. He was curled up sleeping, but yawned and stretched, standing up and looking at me.

"What's this? Breakfast? And no one thought to invite me? How very dare you!"

"You ate before you left our room!" Lizzy shouted at him.

"That's beside the point," Artemis hopped down from the chair, jumped onto my lap and started circling. I gave him an affectionate scritch behind the ear. "I require at least three breakfasts if I want to make it to lunch without an attitude. Chelsea will tell you as much."

"It's true, and he won't shut up until it happens either, it's best to just give into his demands."

"You're too soft on him," Glenda said. Despite this she magicked up a bowl of cat food with her free hand, Artemis jumped down onto the floor and began devouring the food before the metal bowl had finished spinning into place.

"I wonder if the events of last night are going to effect the wedding?" Lizzy asked. "Sorry Chelsea, I don't mean to stress you out."

"Hey, I'm not stressed. Gloria is the one planning everything, wherever she is. I'm paying her to take my stress."

"Besides Chelsea couldn't ask for a better vacation if she tried," Glenda said. "She's tripped over a dead body, so she can cross that off her list."

"And there's also the case of this missing freight container," Deacon pointed out.

"Yes, yes, there are mysteries everywhere. Stop teasing now. I already told you all I'm not getting involved!" I insisted. Everyone laughed at this.

"Hold the phone," Artemis said, lifting his head to take a break to breathe. "You stumbled across another dead body? For real?"

"Yes, yes, hurry up and get the jokes out the way, then we'll move on with the morning."

"I don't have any jokes, I'd never make fun of you, Chelsea. I'm your dear familiar! I know this vacation and time with Deacon is what's most valuable to you. You're getting married!"

"Thanks Artemis. See?" I said to the others. "Someone has my back."

"Plus, if you use this vacation to do any more mystery solving Deacon might just split up with you, though that might not be such a bad thing—you *could* cover more ground that way," Artemis joked. At this Lizzy almost spit out her drink and Glenda about choked on her bacon. Even Deacon was laughing.

"Sorry," Deacon said. "It *was* pretty funny."

"I guess," I said letting out an exasperated sigh, trying not to show my amusement.

"I had to Chelsea, sorry, you'll forgive me right. Can we go down to the pool today? Lizzy won't take me. She says that people 'wouldn't like it' if they saw a cat strolling around the pool of a luxury hotel."

"I think I have to side with Lizzy on this one, sorry furball. Most people don't bring their pets on vacation."

"I could be there in my astral form, right? I just want to sit back and soak up those Hawaiian rays. I'd have to make sure my stuff is securely stored in the room's safe first though. I brought my vintage baseball cards, don't want those babies getting stolen by some sticky-fingered hotel staff, you know I saw this documentary and it said that—"

"Alabama lamas! That's it" I gasped, standing up from the table as the answer came to me.

"Not heard that one before," Glenda muttered.

I looked at Deacon. "The numbers at the end of the suicide note. They're the combination for a safe!"

"That... *does* make sense," Deacon said. "You should probably go and tell them."

"Come with me!" I said. "We're on vacation *together*, I'm not doing this without you. Besides, you're a cop! The more the merrier!"

"Eh, what the heck," he said with a shrug. "I'd be lying if I said I wasn't interested."

"We'll come too!" Glenda said. "The mouth and the muscle!"

"Wait, am I the mouth?" Lizzy said in confusion.

"Hey, don't leave me out, if you're all going, I'll come too. Put me back in that locket. It's time to solve some mysteries baby!" Artemis howled.

* * *

THE PARTY FILED into the elevator, and we rode it to the top floor. As the doors opened, I saw two of the island police sitting at a table playing cards, they looked up at us. They were both large-bellied men. "Hey guys, we need to see your ID's and room keys. What room are you in?" one of them asked.

"None of us are on this floor," I explained. "Is Sunny around? I helped out last night, and I think I've had a revelation about the crime scene."

"Ah, you must be the sleuth lady," the other officer said. "Sunny said you'd be back." He pulled out a phone and made a call. "Chief, yeah, she's here. Okay—alright—yeah, no worries." He put the phone away again. "He'll be up in a minute. Who are the rest of you?"

"This is Deacon, my fiancé," I explained. "He's a cop."

"And the other two?"

"Glenda Sponks, amateur muscle for hire," Glenda said. "This here is Lizzy Sponks, she's my assistant."

"Why do I have to be the assistant?" Lizzy said, turning to look at Glenda. "Ignore her, I'm Lizzy Sponks, sidekick extraordinaire, this here is Glenda—she's feral."

"Uh huh…" the cop said with an uncertain expression. "I'll have to ask the two of you to head back down. Sleuth lady and her fiancé can come through. You two are not welcome, sorry."

"Prejudice!" Glenda said as Deacon and I stepped out of the elevator. "Just because I'm a woman of larger stature!"

"I guess we'll go and enjoy our vacation?" Lizzy suggested to Glenda. Glenda seemed to get over the idea of being left out very quickly. She smiled, shrugged, hit the close door button and stuck her tongue out at us as she disappeared from sight.

A few minutes later Sunny Saupo arrived. The cops guarding the elevators had us wait in the corridor until he did.

"Ah, the couple to be!" Sunny said warmly as he stepped out of the elevator. "I had a funny feeling I'd be seeing you again, Miss Sponks."

"You did?" I asked. Sunny started in the direction of the room, and we followed him.

"Yes, that's your thing, isn't it? A sleuth can't let go of a question until they have an answer. I dare say you were up all night figuring it out. I'm guessing you've figured out the numbers at the end of the letter."

"As a matter of fact, I think I have. Don't tell me you've already done it?"

"Nope, we're all stumped, but I was up late pondering it over. Tell me, how did you figure it out?" Sunny unlocked the door. We ducked through the police tape zigzagging the frame and entered the room. It felt quiet and empty now and looking through into the bedroom I could see the body was now gone.

"I don't know really, it just kind of came to me over breakfast—I slept quite well actually."

"Well don't leave us in suspense any longer," Sunny said keenly. "What do the numbers mean?"

"They're the combination to a safe, most likely the safe in *this* room," I explained.

Sunny blinked, looking as though he felt stupid for not figuring that out earlier. "I'm guessing the safe is in the wardrobe, let's go and put your theory to the test."

The three of us walked into the now-vacant bedroom. The bed had been stripped bare, even the mattress was gone. A walk in a wardrobe was over on the right-hand side of the room, and inside there was a built-in safe near the floor. Sunny crouched down and looked back at me.

"Remind me of the combination again?" he said and put on a pair of gloves.

"3839," I prompted.

"Here goes nothing," he said repeating the code out loud as he punched it into the keypad. "3839." The safe door clicked open, and Sunny looked back at me with a keen glint in his eye. "It seems your talents have not gone to waste, Miss Sponks!" he said excitedly.

Sunny opened the door properly and at first glance my heart sank, as I thought the safe was completely empty. He reached in however and pulled out three brown envelopes that were unsealed. "It's a will and testament," he said as he pulled out the contents of the first envelope. "To my wife, January Roberts, I leave everything to you, and you alone."

"Looks like the wife cleaned up then," Deacon surmised. Sunny put the will back in its envelope, placed it back in the safe and examined the contents of the second envelope.

"It's… another will and testament," Sonny glanced at me, one brow lifted slightly in question. "To my friend, Doctor Herman Klaus, I leave everything to you, and you alone."

"Hold on a second," I said. "Doesn't that directly contradict the first will and testament?"

The three of us shared a look with one another. Sunny put the second will back in the safe and opened up the last envelope. "Anybody want to place bets on what's inside this?" he asked. Lo and behold he pulled out another identical set of legal documents. Another will and testament. He cleared his throat and read it out loud. "To my son, Callum Roberts, I leave everything to you, and you alone."

Sunny placed the third will back in its envelope and set if in the safe with the other two. "So, we have three will and testaments, all in direct contradiction with one another, all found because of the code left at the end of Victor's suicide note," Deacon said, thinking out loud.

"What do you think?" Sunny asked the both of us. "He drafted three documents, and he was going to pick one person—but perhaps left all three in the safe by accident."

"Are they all signed, witnessed, and dated?" I asked.

"A good question!" Sunny said. He quickly pulled each will back out again and checked each one in turn—sure enough they were all signed, witnessed, and dated—all on the same date too—three days ago.

"Who are the witnesses?" Deacon asked. There were two names on each document, each different. "Do you recognize them?

"Vaguely," Sunny said. "I think the six witnesses are all people that work for Victor's hotel. I know at least three of them, and the other three I'm pretty sure. Here's the part I don't understand, if Victor planned to kill himself then why would he leave three contradictory wills for us to find?"

"Something about it doesn't make sense, that's for sure," Deacon said. He looked over at me. "What do you make of all this?"

"It's very confusing," I said. "By the way Sunny, did you get any results back from the lab and the autopsy yet?"

"Yes! Sorry, I should have told you as soon as I saw you. The autopsy came back as positive for morphine overdose. It looks like dear old Victor popped the pills and died around fifteen minutes later. The maid discovered him shortly after."

So that confirmed it then. The science told us it was a morphine overdose, and the mysterious note found in Victor's hand had now led to this confusing spectacle—three identical wills that were in direct contradiction with one another.

There was one thing clear in this mystery so far—there were plenty of unanswered questions.

CHAPTER 8

"What happens to the estate if there are multiple wills that contradict one another?" I asked Deacon, who shrugged in response.

"I'm not entirely sure, maybe the estate gets split between those three people?" He looked at Sunny for an answer.

"My memory is a little hazy, but I believe each of the wills would be nullified. I don't know what would happen to the money in that case. I deal with the law, not the fineries of estate planning like this!"

I walked back into the bedroom with my hands clasped behind my back, pacing as I tried to figure things out. I put myself in Victor Robert's position. Let's say I had three people I cared about in my life, Deacon, Lizzy, and Glenda. Should I die, I would like some of my money to go to each of them. If I thought they were important to mention as the sole heir of my entire estate—which admittedly wasn't that much—then why would I also completely exclude them on another document and leave the money to someone else?

"Was he senile?" I asked, pivoting around on my heels to look at Sunny. "Of his right mind?"

"As far as I know," Sunny said. "I spoke with Victor a few times a week, and he's always seemed pretty lucid to me. There's nothing out of the ordinary on his medical records from what we've found, he wasn't on any regular medication, not even anti-depressants."

"It seems likely a man that felt suicidal would have been prescribed anti-depressants at some point," Deacon said.

"Yes," I agreed, "and let's be honest Sunny, did he seem suicidal to you? I spoke with the man in the elevator only hours before he died, and he was talking about wanting several more decades. He had a zeal for life by all accounts."

Sunny nodded in thoughtful agreement. "I agree this course of action seems most unlikely from a man of Victor Roberts' stature, but I'm afraid the science can't lie. My forensic and coroner, Jill, said his blood contained fatal levels of morphine, and they even found it in the water glass on the bedside table too."

That little tidbit made me turn my head in attention. "Hold the phone, it was in his drinking glass? Trace amounts or a heavy saturation?"

Sunny shrugged. "Does it matter?"

"Terribly so!" I shouted. "Don't you understand? I need to speak to this forensic of yours. Do you have a phone number for her? I'd like to talk with her at once. I think we should also speak with each of the people mentioned in these wills, see if they know about the contradictory documents."

"Good idea," Sunny said. "I'll also make sure these wills are put into sealed evidence straightaway. Don't want them getting destroyed. If only one remains, then that person becomes the de facto receiver of the entire estate!"

"There will be copies at the legal office that drafted the documents," I said. "I wouldn't worry too much about that." Sunny passed me the information for swiss-army-knife forensic Jill, who was also the island coroner. I called her immediately and after three rings someone answered the phone.

"Diamond Island Coroner's office, this is Roger speaking, how may I help?"

"This is Chelsea Sponks," I said. "May I speak with Jill please?"

"She's currently shoulder deep in a cadaver," Roger said plainly. "Is there something I can help you with? I'm her assistant."

"It's with regards to the Victor Roberts' case, I had some questions about the evidence."

"Oh?" Roger said, his voice breaking slightly. "Uh, well I'm not at liberty to discuss things like that with civilians."

Sunny, who had heard Roger's response through the phone's speaker, rolled his eyes and held out his hand. I passed him the phone. "Roger? Yeah, it's Sunny here, Sunny Saupo. Just a quick note to let you know that Miss Sponks has my blessing to work on the case. I've deputized her, okay? Now tell the woman what she wants to know, alright? Alright."

I took the phone back from Sunny, thanking him as I did so. "Roger? Me again. I wanted to know about the glass of water found on Victor Robert's bedside table. Sunny mentioned you found morphine in the water?"

"That's… right," Roger said.

"What made you think to test the water in the first place?"

"It's fairly standard procedure to test all food and drink found at a scene, especially when an overdose is suspected," Roger answered.

"And what was the conclusion? How much morphine was in the water? Are we talking a small amount here, like residual pill powder from his lips or fingers?"

"No, it was a substantial amount," Roger clarified. "Like the pills had been dissolved into the water."

"What about prints?" I asked. "On the glass?"

"Curiously enough there was only one set of prints on the glass, *and* on the box of tablets found in the trash can we found two—one set matched the prints on the glass, the other prints are unknown—probably from the employee at the drug store, if I was guessing."

"And the prints on the glass and the pill box, they belonged to Victor Roberts?"

"No," Roger said. "We don't have an identification on those yet. Oh, Jill's here now! Jill, it's that detective woman from last night, she wanted to know about the results."

"Hello?" Jill's voice came as she took the phone. "Miss Sponks, right? What did you want to know?"

"To be honest I think I've heard everything I need to know. The water was spiked, and Victor's prints weren't on the pills, or the glass of water, is that right?"

"Yes, I said as much in the report that I sent over to Sunny."

"One moment," I said, holding the phone to my shoulder and looking at Sunny. "Sunny, Jill said she's already given you this information in a report, is that right?"

"Huh?" Sunny said, breaking out of a trance—he was staring at the wall ahead of him. "Oh yes, she did. Lots of big technical words though, I tend to zone out around that sort of thing. I think the gist was that Roberts killed himself though, right?"

I shook my head. "No, that's not what the evidence is saying at all." I put the phone back to my ear. "Jill, are you still there?"

"I am," she affirmed. "Is there anything else I can help you with?"

"Yes, I think I've already drawn a conclusion myself based off your scientific evidence, but I want to hear your opinion of the case. What happened to Victor Roberts?"

"In my scientific opinion?" she asked, her voice wavering a little. "Victor Roberts' drink was spiked with a fatal amount of morphine, and he did not touch the glass. I don't think this is a suicide at all, I think this is a murder. We find the owner of those mystery prints and we have our killer. I'm guessing your assessment is similar?"

"Exactly the same," I said with a satisfied smile. "Thanks Jill, I'll be in touch." With that I hung up the phone and looked at Sheriff Sunny. "Sheriff, are you keeping up?"

"Spell it out for me, Sponks, I didn't get much sleep last night."

"This isn't a suicide, Sunny. We're dealing with a murder case here."

* * *

SUNNY LOOKED SHOCKED at the revelation. At the same time there was a spark in his eyes, like a man that had been waiting for this moment all his life. "You're kidding me! But this is wonderful!" Sunny paused for a moment upon hearing himself. "I mean… *terrible.* This is terrible."

"You might want to work on that reaction before other people see it," I recommended. "But yes, there you have it—it looks like Victor Roberts didn't kill himself, someone did this to him."

"Which means the suicide note is a forgery," Deacon surmised.

"Meaning that the killer *wanted* us to find the three contradictory wills inside the safe!" Sunny said with an excitable squeak. "But… it still doesn't explain why there are three wills."

"Chelsea, would you like to hear my quick take?" Deacon asked me.

"Always my darling, butter up my ears with your beautiful intelligence."

Deacon smirked. "When we first met Victor Roberts, I remember him saying he was an 'all or nothing' kind of guy. What if he decided to leave his entire estate to one person, but hadn't yet decided who he was going to leave it to? That would explain the three wills."

"Deacon you're so smart, I think I could marry you," I joked.

"I'm afraid I don't follow," Sunny Saupo said.

"Don't you see?" Deacon asked. "If Victor confided in each of these three people that they were named in his will, then it stands to reason that each of these people is a suspect. We need to speak with each of them individually and see what they knew—but they cannot know about the wills. If Victor told each of them they would be the sole heir, then that person has a mighty fine motive to murder him. The man was worth a lot of money after all."

"I understand!" Sunny said, smiling broadly at Deacon's explanation. He looked over at the bedside table and pouted thoughtfully. "You know my money would be on the wife, after all the prescription was in her name."

"Where is January Roberts?" I asked. "I saw her leaving the hotel last night."

"She returned to the island this morning, we contacted her about her husband's passing."

"And we know that Doctor Herman Klaus is definitely in the hotel, and I met Victor's son, Callum, just the other day, so he's here somewhere too."

"How exciting!" Sunny said, he composed himself then simmered down a little. "I mean… I will round up the suspects and we can talk to them individually. I will… try and stay calm."

"See that you do, Sunny," I advised. "See that you do."

THE FIRST PERSON we met with was Doctor Herman Klaus, who was in his bedroom, only a few doors down. After knocking on the door, he welcomed us inside after we asked to talk.

"Let us sit at the table on the balcony," the doctor said. When we were all sitting the conversation proceeded. "So, what do you want to know?" he asked.

"Did Victor ever speak with you about his estate?" I asked him. "My understanding is that you are old friends. I even heard you loaned Victor money to help him start the hotel."

"That is correct," the doctor answered. "Back then Victor was just a poor man with a dream, but now he is far richer than I could ever dream—I mean, he *was* far richer."

"How are you taking the passing of your friend, doctor?" Deacon asked. From where I was sitting the middle-aged man didn't seem too emotionally fraught.

"Rest assured I am devastated," he answered, "but I'm not the kind that wears my heart on my sleeve. What was it you wanted to know about his estate?"

"Did he ever mention it to you?" I asked. "Share the details of his will?"

Herman Klaus' lips pressed together in a tight line; he took a quick sip of his drink then set the cup back down on the table. "You're asking, so I'm guessing that you already know, you must have found something. What have you found?"

"What did he tell you?" I said, batting the ball back in his court.

Klaus considered me for a moment, his eyes sharp and shrewd. I could tell he didn't like being the one in the interview chair, but his curiosity got the better of him. "Victor confided in me privately a few weeks ago, he said he was going to include me in his will and testament, as thanks for my friendship and support over the years."

"Did he specify what the arrangement of the will would be?" Deacon probed.

The doctor shook his head. "No, only that I would be named. What have you found? It had something to do with that bible verse, didn't it?"

"...No," I said, almost having completely forgotten about the doctor's unusual infatuation with the bible verse. "There is a will, and you are named in it—as the sole heir."

Herman Klaus just about spit his drank out. "You're kidding! Everything? Dear god!"

"That surprises you, doctor?" Sunny Saupo asked keenly.

"Yes, of course! I mean when Victor mentioned I was in the will I expected something, but not everything!" He paused for a moment then looked at me astutely. "Now hold on a moment, I think I'm intelligent enough to follow the line of questioning here. Are you suggesting I had something to do with Victor's death?"

"Did you?" I asked plainly.

Doctor Herman Klaus pulled back his head as though offended with the suggestion. "Are you out of your mind? He's one of my oldest friends! And it was a suicide!" A few seconds passed and then his expression changed. "It *was* a suicide, wasn't it?"

"The mounting evidence is beginning to suggest the contrary. I'm sorry but we can't say much more than that right now. As of this moment though we'll have to ask you to remain in your room, Doctor Klaus, you are officially a person of interest in this investigation."

"Investigation?!" Klaus said in surprise. He stood up from the table as we did, moral outrage evident on his face. "You have no right to talk to me like this! What reason do you have!"

"Are you not a specialist in poisoning?" I asked him. "You told me yourself you are a world-leading expert when it comes to toxicology."

"Yes, and? So what?"

"I find it highly suspicious you just happen to be here at the hotel the same week your oldest friend dies from a drug overdose—and you are named as the sole beneficiary of his estate. Not only that but you are even staying on the same floor as him, and I dare say you had readily available access to the man. I'm sorry doctor but you have to look at things from where we're standing, your presence is highly suspicious given the circumstances, and from this point on you will be treated as a suspect."

"I want my lawyer!" Klaus demanded, to no one in particular.

"Sunny, get this man his lawyer, and get a fingerprinting kit too, I want to run his prints against the scene."

"I was just about to suggest the same thing!" Sunny said with a warm smile.

CHAPTER 9

The next person we met with was January Roberts, who had arrived back at the hotel that morning. Sunny arranged for the four of us to sit down and talk on a quiet part of the patio.

We were already waiting at the table when January Roberts arrived, escorted by a couple of Sunny's officers. The small blonde was wearing large black shades, and underneath those shades I could tear-streaked eyeliner down her cheeks.

"So?" she asked as she took a seat at the table. She lit a cigarette and blew out smoke, opting to keep her shades on. It wasn't particularly sunny at the moment and the sky was quite overcast, so she could only be trying to keep her eyes hidden. "What is the nature of this meeting?"

"Where did you go last night?" I asked. "You left the hotel."

January leaned forward and flicked ash into a glass, taking another drag before she answered. "I was staying with a friend on the mainland."

"Which friend?" Deacon asked.

"That doesn't matter," January replied. "I got back this morning just after nine."

"How are you holding up?" I queried. "Forgive me if I'm stating the obvious, but it looks like the news has hit you hard."

January almost looked incredulous at the comment. "Of course, the news has hit me hard. My husband is dead, and at his own hand at that! When I left here last night, I hardly expected that would be the last time I'd see him alive!"

That was reasonable. "I'm assuming Victor talked with you about his last will and testament?" I asked.

"Is that what this meeting is about?" she asked. "Shouldn't the lawyers be here?"

"This is just an informal conversation," I clarified, "not a legal proceeding. What did you know about his will?"

"Not much," she said after a moment of consideration. "He said he would take care of me in the event of his passing. He mentioned I was part of the will—"

"What about all of it?" Deacon interrupted.

January looked rocked by the news. "I beg your pardon?"

"He named you as the sole heir for the entire thing," Sunny said, stepping into the conversation. "What do you make of that, Mrs. Roberts?"

January sputtered. "I—I don't know what to say, that is most unexpected."

"As unexpected as Victor killing himself? You were his wife, you probably knew him better than most, did he express that he felt suicidal?"

"Not at all!" January proclaimed. "He would never!"

"But yet…" Sunny interjected.

"Victor would never kill himself. I don't care what it looks like, it's not right!"

"You are correct," I told her. "It looks like a suicide, but the evidence suggests it was staged."

"So, this is a murder?" January said, her mouth hanging slightly agape.

I nodded. "That is our suspicion, yes."

She drew back a little. "Then I am a suspect," she concluded.

"Why would you say that?" Deacon asked.

"You found a will declaring me the sole heir of the estate. You doubt the suicide—just as I do, I dare say you're gunning to have me in the gallows before the sunsets today!" January dramatically stubbed her cigarette in her ash tray and held her wrists out over the table. "Just do it then!"

"Do what?" I asked, feeling slightly bemused by her dramatic reaction.

"Arrest me, if that's what you came here to do!"

"No one is under arrest—yet—" Sunny clarified. "Mrs. Roberts, please do not get upset, we're merely trying to get the facts straight. Miss Sponks?"

"Mrs. Roberts it looks like Victor died of a morphine overdose—likely from the oxycontin tablets we found in his trash. Those tablets were prescribed to you, picked up from the pharmacy yesterday."

Despite the large shades I could see confusion appear on her face. "No, that can't be right. I didn't go to the pharmacy yesterday."

"What is the prescription for?" Deacon probed.

"Back pain. A hangover from an old skiing accident." January opened the large designer handbag resting on her lap and pulled out an identical box of pills. "This box is practically already full; I didn't go to the pharmacy yesterday because I don't need any more tablets!"

Deacon inspected the box and sure enough it was almost full.

"But we have the other box," Sunny said. "It has your name on it, and it's dated yesterday."

"Then it's wrong," January snapped. "I didn't go to the pharmacy yesterday. Heck, I haven't been in over a month!" Deacon, Sunny and I all exchanged a silent look with one another. "I'm telling the truth!" January shouted again.

"Very well," I said, standing to leave. "If possible, we'd like to get your prints, and you'll need to stay on the island. Don't go anywhere, no more late-night trips."

"As if I have time. I have a funeral to plan!" January said in exasperation, lighting another cigarette as I prepared to leave. I wasn't sure what to make of my encounter with the unusual woman. Unlike the doctor she was visibly distraught over the whole ordeal, or she was faking it and in the running for an acting award of the highest order.

"Have you tracked down the son yet?" I asked Sunny as we left.

"Yes, but are we not wasting our time here? It seems so obvious to me that it was the wife!" Sunny proclaimed.

"Maybe, but let's see what the son has to say first."

SUNNY'S MEN tracked Callum Roberts to the beach, where we found him swimming in the water. As we walked out onto the shore, Sunny signaled Callum from the sand, who noticed him after a minute of trying. He walked out of the water, took a towel from a chair on the sand and came over to us, a confused expression on his face.

"What's this about?"

"We were hoping we could talk to you," I said. Callum dried his face off, he was a little red from the excursion of swimming, and slightly out of breath too.

"About what happened to father?"

"Yes. How are you holding up?" I asked. Looking at him his eyes were swollen as though he had been crying recently.

"I'm not going to lie, I've been better. To be honest I think I'm still in shock. I came out here to try and clear my head. Dad, kill himself? I just… I just can't believe it."

"What if I told you we don't believe it either?" I asked. "The evidence suggests the suicide was staged, and that someone did it to him."

Callum looked completely shocked, and also angry. He turned his attention to Sheriff Saupo. "Is that true, Sheriff? You think he was murdered?"

"Yes son," Sunny said apologetically. "Sorry you had to hear this way."

"Who did it?" Callum asked. "I'll kill the son of a b—"

"We don't know," I said honestly. "But we're trying to get to the bottom of it."

"It was her, wasn't it? That vampire, January. Please tell me you've arrested her. Everyone knows she only ever wanted one thing out of him? She's a leech, a bloodsucker!" Callum's fists were clenched tightly, and I worried what would happen between him and his stepmother if they crossed paths.

"Just calm down," Deacon said. "There are a few people of note in this case, and I'm sorry to inform you that you might be one of them."

Callum looked offended by that. "Are you kidding me? Me? Kill my own father? For what?!"

"For money," I said simply. "You said yourself that you've been struggling ever since your father cut you off. Tell me, what did he tell you about your inheritance?"

"Inheritance?" Callum scoffed. "Inheritance? What inheritance! I already told you he cut me off, why would I expect anything from him once he was six-feet-under?"

"He's got a point, Sponks," Sunny said to me.

"And how would you react if I told you, you are the sole heir named in his well? You receive everything."

Callum looked thoroughly perplexed by the revelation. "You're kidding me?"

"No," Deacon said. "With the fact that the suicide is called into question and you're the only named recipient, naturally you come under suspicion then as a suspect."

Callum blinked for a moment as he comprehended the information. "That's a load of bull crap! He was my own father! I wouldn't lay a finger on him!"

"You have to see things from our perspective, son," Sunny said calmly. "We're not saying you did it, we're just saying... things don't look good, eh?"

Callum seemed to calm a little at this. "If you really thought I did this you would have brought more people to arrest me, so... what else aren't you telling me?" The three of us looked at one another. Of the people we had spoken to so far Callum was the only one to question our procedure.

"Nothing—" Sunny began, but Callum quickly interrupted.

"You're not being truthful with me. This is a test, you want to see how I react, that's it, isn't?"

"You are correct," I said, seeing no sense in lying to him. "Though what we have told you is true. The suicide has been determined as staged. One tidbit we left out is that multiple wills were found, all in contradiction with one another." Sunny looked at me as though I had betrayed a great secret. "Relax, it was going to come out eventually, makes sense to put it out there while we can."

I quickly recapped the findings to Callum Roberts, who seemed as intrigued and mystified as the rest of us. "Why multiple wills though? Father wasn't one to dwell over things. He made a choice and stuck with it." Callum scratched his head while trying to puzzle things out.

"It seems this particular choice had him stumped," Deacon reasoned.

"How can I help?" Callum asked. "I need to get to the bottom of this."

"Stay on the island, and stay out of trouble," I asked. "As we mentioned you are a person of interest now, and the police will be keeping an eye on you until we figure things out."

"I'll be out here, minding my own business," Callum said. "I want you to find out who killed my father, Miss Sponks."

"That's what I intend to do, don't you worry. Oh, we'll need some prints off you by the way, one of Sheriff's Saupo's men will be along shortly to sort that out."

"Of course, whatever I can do to help the investigation."

With that, Deacon, Sunny, and I made our way back to the hotel. So far, we had spoken with each of the people named in the wills, and each person had responded a little differently. Doctor Herman Klaus didn't seem too beaten up about losing his life-long friend, but he did mention that emotion wasn't a strong suit of his.

January, seen as a gold-digging wife by many of the staff, did appear to be genuinely upset about the loss of her husband, and Victor's estranged son, Callum, looked like he was struggling as well. Sunny was convinced January had something to do with it as the pills that killed her husband were in her name, but I wasn't so sure—for one she was gone last night. Establishing a time of death would certainly help us figure out if Victor Roberts died before or after his wife left the hotel.

Whoever did this stood to inherit a lot of money, but there were several elements of the crime scene that just didn't make sense in my mind—though I couldn't yet quite articulate why.

"That about settles it for me," Sunny said as we headed back inside. The police had set up a temporary HQ in the office behind the lobby, we went through into their temporary workspace and Sunny slumped down behind a desk, put his hands behind his head and threw his legs up. "The wife is the one that did it!"

"How can you be so sure?" I asked. "We haven't learned anything meaningful yet."

"No, but I have a gift for these things, I guess you can call it police-man's intuition. It's her, you'll see."

I made an unsure face. "How long will it take to get these prints processed?"

"The doctor and the wife are already done; we just need to get the son. Once we have them, I'll get one of my men to run the prints back to the station and see what comes up. Now that I think about it, I should check in at the pharmacy too, see if I can establish whether January Roberts was there or not yesterday—she obviously *was*, of course."

"Taking sides, Sheriff?" I said curiously.

Sunny seemed to take heed of my observation and lifted his hands in the air. "You know what Sponks you're right, I should cool off a little until we get more evidence, eh? Sorry about that—bad police-work. I'm just excited, this is our island's first ever murder-mystery!"

Sunny's phone started ringing and he answered it. "Hello? Oh, hi Kev, how you doing buddy? Really? How absolutely bizarre. Luggage? But what happened to the fish? That's a strange one—"

Deacon and I, unable to avoid overhearing the conversation, looked at one another as we pieced together the other end of the phone call. Upon checking in here we'd received frozen fish instead of our luggage.

"You don't think?" Deacon muttered to me.

"Sunny!" I said, causing him to hold the phone against his shoulder. "Yes, Sponks? You can uh… go for now if you like, I don't suppose this thread will move until we get the prints back."

"Actually, your phone call has my interest. What's this about luggage and fish?"

"Oh, you'll love this one! It's my friend Kevin, he's the head chef at the kitchen over at the Blue Lagoon hotel on the mainland. He just called with a bit of a pickle; he was expecting a shipment of fish the other day but instead he got luggage. Talk about a funny one!"

"I think that's one mystery we might be able to solve," I said.

"Oh?" Sunny asked, turning his head in interest.

"Yeah, that luggage belongs to us." I turned and looked at Deacon.

"You don't say!" Sunny said in amused bewilderment. "Well… I can arrange a boat to take you over there and pick it up. Say, wasn't that matchbook you found on the beach for The Blue Lagoon? You guys can investigate that missing freight container while you're over there!"

Deacon gave me a disinterested look, one that I felt myself mirroring. "I uh… yeah. Yeah, I guess we can check it out quickly while we're over there," I said. It seemed like this vacation wasn't starting anytime soon.

We made our way down to the beach, where a small white schooner let down its anchor to pick us up and take us to the Hawaiian mainland. Even though this wasn't exactly how I'd pictured us spending our time here in paradise, I had to admit it was nice to get out and admire the scenery with Deacon—even if we technically were working.

Crystal clear water lapped up against the boat, a warm azure syrup that sparkled under the golden sun. Deacon and I climbed on board, made ourselves comfortable and held on tight as the small boat took off across the ocean, leaving Diamond Island behind us.

"What takes you to the mainland?" the captain asked from the ship's wheel. There were a few other people on the boat, but we were spaced out enough for private conversation.

"Missing luggage… and a missing freight container too, I guess," I said. The captain offered me a confused look.

"You're the woman helping Sunny, aren't you? Whole island is talking about you, you've got everybody interested. People saying the old man killed himself, but I've heard rumors it's not that straightforward." The captain said the whole thing as a statement, but with a questioning tone underneath.

"I'm not a liberty to discuss that right now."

One thing was clear though, the gossip travelled around this island, and it travelled fast.

Forty minutes later the Hawaiian mainland came into view, a small shape that crept over the horizon and grew in size until it seemed massive. The boat docked, we tipped the captain and followed his directions to the Blue Lagoon, which wasn't far from the coast.

After ten minutes of walking, we arrived at the front doors of the Blue Lagoon, a four-story building with white walls and palm trees bordering its luscious green grounds. We headed inside, breathing a sigh of relief as air conditioning enveloped us once more.

"Aloha, welcome to the Blue Lagoon," a young woman with a pearlescent smile said as we reached the desk. "Are you checking in today?"

"Looking for luggage," I said. "We were told to ask for Kevin."

"Of course! You will find Kevin in the kitchen. May I ask who I'm speaking with?"

"Chelsea and Deacon Sponks. Sunny Saupo sent us."

"Ah, yes, Sunny—quite the character, isn't he? Let me call Kevin and check he's free." The receptionist made a quick call and then placed the phone down again. "You're in luck. If you follow signs for the restaurant, you'll find him there. Have a good day now."

We followed the signs to the restaurant, and when we arrived there, we found it empty apart from one large Hawaiian man who was behind a bar, sharpening knives. "Quiet now, but it'll be packed in here later! You must be the owners of the mysterious luggage that turned up, I'm Kevin, the head-chef here at The Blue Lagoon. Your luggage is on the table there behind you."

Deacon and I turned in the direction Kevin pointed and saw our suitcases on the table of an empty booth. We both let out a sigh of relief to finally be reunited with our luggage. "We can't tell you how thankful we are," Deacon said. "How did this happen in the first place?"

Kevin just laughed and shrugged his shoulders. "Wish I could tell you buddy. I was as stumped as you. Still haven't got my fish, the airline must have messed up with their luggage manifest or something. I'll have to bill them for it! Do you guys want something to eat while you're here? I can rustle up a nice pulled pork sandwich?"

"That would be... amazing," I said, my whole mouth having filled with saliva just at the mention of pulled pork. Ten minutes later the two of us were eating amazing sandwiches with a glass of sparkling lemonade.

"I might be exaggerating," Deacon said," but that is the *best* sandwich I have ever eaten.

Kevin, who was still sharpening knives behind the bar threw his head back and laughed heartily. "Glad to be of service! Sunny mentioned you were both helping him with the Victor Roberts suicide over on Diamond Island? I have to say that was surprising to hear, I never knew he was struggling with something like that."

"Evidence suggests it was staged anyway—" I said, giving up pretense of keeping the secret any longer. It seemed like everybody else on the island already knew anyway.

"Yeah, I'd heard as much," Kevin said with an astute nod. "Sunny said you're some superstar sleuth or something. I dare say you'll have it all sorted in no time."

"That's kind of you to say, thank you. I'm not so sure though, honestly, we just came here to get married. We weren't expecting any of this!"

"We should ask about the container, while we're here," Deacon said between bites of his sandwich.

"Container?" Kevin asked.

"There's this uh... freight container," I said. "Its contents are valuable, and the container vanished yesterday morning from Diamond Island. It looks like a boat picked it up off the beach."

"Oh?" Kevin said, putting down his knives. "And you think it might be here?"

"We have no idea where it is," Deacon said. "To be honest it's a freight container, it's kind of difficult to hide that sort of thing."

Kevin laughed. "Very true."

"We found a matchbook for the Blue Lagoon," I said. "On the sand where the freight container had been. Is there anyone who works here at the hotel who can sail a boat and smokes?"

Kevin thought about it for a moment then nodded. "You know I can think of two people actually, my line chef, Oli, he smokes like a chimney, and he used to be in the Navy—but I think the more likely option is Hiroto."

"Hiroto?" Deacon asked.

"Yeah, he's this old Japanese dude, he's got a tugger that does a lot of the delivery routes between the islands. He handles most of the shipments that come into the hotel."

"Do you know where we could find him?"

"Hiroto? Sure, he lives in a shack down by the beach. I can walk you over if you like, I'm heading that way anyhow—I need to pick up some muscles."

Deacon and I followed the large Hawaiian man on the short walk from The Blue Lagoon to the beach. As we reached the sand, he held a hand over his eyes to shield out the sun and pointed down the beach. "That's Hiroto's hut down there. He'll be in, but he will be sleeping most likely. If I were you, I'd go bearing gifts—he won't be happy with a wakeup call."

I looked at the dilapidated shack. "What do I get the man that already has anything?"

Kevin mimed drinking from a bottle. "Hiroto likes his tipple. You can't go wrong with that. Anyhow, I'm going to pick up these muscles. Make sure you grab your luggage before y'all head back to Diamond Island, and hey—best of luck with the case! ...And the wedding!"

Deacon and I started down the sand, heading in the direction of the dilapidated beach hut. "What about this gift?" Deacon asked. "Should we go and get something in town?"

"Following Kevin's recommendations, yes—" I didn't want to be dealing with a grumpy alcoholic Japanese fisherman today, "but let's speed things up a little."

After checking the coast was clear—it was—I magicked up a gift for Hiroto, it was a bottle of fancy-looking sake.

"Nice," Deacon remarked. "Hey… something I've always wondered.

Where does that come from anyway? Like, how does it work? Did that just appear out of nowhere?"

"No. Whatever shop was nearest. The bottle will disappear from there, and my money will appear in the register, almost like I was in the shop."

"Doesn't that freak out the mortals?" Deacon asked.

"I think magic has a way of covering things, so people don't notice," I said. "I mean I could take the bottle for free if I wanted, but I'm not a thief. You can go crazy wondering how all this magic stuff works." Lord knows I almost certainly had when first learning. "The best thing to do is just accept it and move on."

Deacon nodded in agreement. We reached the dilapidated shack and Deacon knocked on the door. After a moment of silence there came the sound of slurred Japanese grumbling, followed by broken English.

"Who there?!" came the gravelly voice.

"This is Deacon Long and Chelsea Sponks," Deacon said. "We come baring gifts, sorry to wake you at this hour." The sound of unco-ordinated movement came from within the shack, followed by heavy footsteps. A second later the door opened and standing before us was an older Japanese man with a scraggly beard and messy hair.

"What you want?!" he said, squinting at the sunlight.

"We just wanted to ask you a few questions," I said. "We brought you this." I held up the bottle of sake and Hiroto's eyes lit up. He snatched the bottle from me and grinned like a child in a candy store.

"Now you I like! Ask away? You wanna drink?"

"We're... good," I said. "Is there any chance you picked up a freight container yesterday morning from Diamond Island? It was on the beach outside The Lazy Caw."

"Yes," Hiroto said straightaway. Deacon and I both took note at once.

"Where did you take it?" Deacon asked.

"Back to port," Hiroto said. He uncorked the bottle of sake, smelled it and nodded approvingly. "Container empty. Delivery done."

"The container had something valuable inside," I remarked.

"No," Hiroto said. "Empty. Doors open. No tags on door. I closed them myself. Back at port now. Probably halfway to china with pallets of rum. Delicious rum!"

"You're saying the container was empty when you picked it up?" Deacon asked.

"That's a right," Hiroto said.

"Under whose instruction did you collect the container?" I asked.

Hiroto thought for a moment then held up a finger. He disappeared inside the shack and came back a moment holding a dog-eared ledger. With the bottle of sake still in one hand he thumbed through the ledger before stopping on a page. The old sailor gave a nod of his head, turned the book around and pointed at the entry. He read it out loud as I examined the writing.

"Collect empty, Diamond Island. Return to port." Hiroto tapped the paper. "See? Easy job. Hiroto best sailor in Hawaiian seas. Hiroto no scared of sharks!"

"Who told you to collect the container though?" Deacon repeated. Hiroto jabbed his finger at a cell next to one he had just read.

"Hiroto document everything! Hiroto have to for insurance purposes. Hiroto no like bureaucrats, but Hiroto follows the rules. Hiroto no go back to japan… every customer must provide address and contact number."

Sure enough there was an address and contact number. *345 Rokeo Drive,* followed by a mobile number. Deacon pulled out his cell and dialed the number, he shook his head. "Voicemail."

"Is this far away?" I asked Hiroto. He looked at the address and shook his head.

"Five minute in car. Take Hiroto's car! Just bring it back! No parking tickets, Hiroto be very sad."

"You're sure?" I asked in surprise. "You would let a total stranger borrow your car?"

Hiroto ducked inside and a moment later was throwing a pair of keys at me. "You bring sake. You no stranger. Hiroto friend for life. Hiroto no drive though, Hiroto too tired." He leaned out the door and pointed at a rusted station wagon. "There. No parking ticket, please."

With that the drunken Japanese sailor disappeared back inside the shack with a genial grin. Deacon and I stared at each other for a few confused seconds before we started walking over to the rusted station wagon.

"He was… interesting," Deacon said with a smirk. We climbed inside the wagon and started the engine. Deacon typed the address into his phone and gave me directions while I pulled away.

"Odd guy, but he seemed nice enough," I commented. "What do you think we'll find at this address?"

"Answers?" Deacon shrugged. "I'm getting the impression this whole thing was one big mix up. Hiroto said the container was empty when he picked it up, that suggests the valuable cargo was unloaded on Diamond Island."

"Sunny Saupo said it wasn't though," I recollected, following the words with a sigh. "Why did I have it in my head that Hawaii would be relaxing?"

Deacon laughed. "As if you're not enjoying this."

"I suppose that's true."

Ten minutes later we arrived at 345 Rokeo Drive, another desolate property that was on the beach front. This shack made Hiroto's lean-to look like a Hawaiian palace. As we approached the door and knocked it became pretty obvious that no one was living here.

"I think this address might be a burner…" Deacon said, the front door swinging open as he knocked. As it did so we saw there was no back to the property at all. The old building must have come apart in a storm years ago, and in front of us there was beach and ocean.

"So maybe things aren't as straight forward as we assumed," I said. I walked forward to the point where the old wooden floor blended in with the sand. The house looked like it had once been a simple square shape, but the north-eastern quarter had been torn away in whatever storm had come through here. I looked over on the left and saw the exposed and weather-worn contents of an old bedroom. There was a broken bed, a wardrobe that had fallen over many years ago and—

"Is that a coffin?" I said in bewilderment, walking across the sand to get to the old bedroom. Sure enough there was a coffin lying on the floor next to the broken bed. It had been partially obscured, so I hadn't spotted it at first. It was a simple wooden coffin, its lid nailed-shut.

"Unusual," Deacon remarked. "Let me try this number again." Deacon pulled out his phone and dialed the number that had been on Hiroto's manifest. Immediately we heard a muffled ringtone, and we looked at one another as we followed the sound to its source.

"That's coming from inside the coffin… right?" Deacon said in bafflement.

"Stand back, I'm going to open this thing. I really hope there isn't a body inside here." With my hands outstretched I felt for the nails using my magic. Turning my hands over I lifted my palms towards the sky and the nails and coffin lid lifted up off the box. I pushed the coffin over to the side with my powers and let out a sigh of relief at seeing no body.

The coffin was completely empty except for a single cell phone, which was vibrating and ringing against the wood as Deacon attempted to dial it. I crouched down, looked at the phone and stared back at Deacon.

"What in the dickens is going on here?" I said. Never had a mystery left me feeling this confused before.

"I was just thinking the same thing," Deacon said, cancelling his call to the coffin phone. Just as he did that my own phone started ringing. Looking at the screen I saw it was Sunny Saupo.

"Sheriff?" I answered.

"Sponks! Any luck with your luggage?" he asked.

"Yeah, we found it. We also found a lead on the container too, though we've hit another dead end." Literally.

"Hold that thought, Sponks, I've got an exciting update for you. The prints came back, and they belonged to the wife. We got her on the pharmacy cameras too, she picked up the pills. That all but settles it for me, Sponks. The wife did it! January Roberts killed her husband!"

CHAPTER 11

"Look on the bright side," Deacon said as we got back to the hotel. "At least we have our luggage now."

"Well that much is true," I said in agreement. Although our unusual case of the missing freight container had only got more bizarre, at least it looked like the case of Victor Robert's murder had made a few steps forward.

The normal hotel service was now back in order too, the restaurant fully operational. Deacon and I met Lizzy and Glenda for dinner, where we caught them up to speed with our day and its unusual events.

"A phone inside a coffin?" Lizzy said in bemusement. "What is it with this place?"

I shrugged. "I'm just happy to have our luggage back. What have y'all been up to today?"

"Lazing on the beach, staring at the young hunks," Glenda said.

"Not me," Lizzy said. "I've been hiding in my room, staying away from the sun."

"Yeah, Lizzy's been spying on the young hunks from her balcony!" Glenda cackled.

"Was not!" Lizzy said defiantly, her cheeks blushing a little. "Hey, at least this Victor Roberts mystery is sorted now," she said to me, keen to change the topic. "You guys can go back to enjoying the vacation, and the wedding is only a few days away!"

"Yeah, nothing like a murder with a neat line under it!" Glenda said.

"Well, a wobbly line at best," I said. They both shot me confused looks.

"You don't think it's over?" Lizzy asked.

"I think there are still questions that haven't been answered." Questions that made me think there was more than met the eye to this crime. Why was there paint missing from the inside of the window frame? Why were the walls and ceiling slightly darkened? Why was the air-conditioning vent tacky?

"I'd ask, but I don't even want to open that jumbled up mess," Glenda said with an eye roll. "Can't you just be happy someone else solved a murder? It doesn't always have to be you!"

"Believe me, I'm more than happy for other people to take that job, I'm just saying that something doesn't feel right to me—when that happens there's usually a reason."

"Because you're incapable of enjoying yourself!" the astral form of my familiar, Artemis, piped up from a wall beside our table. Only our party could see him. "Let your hair down, enjoy yourself!"

"I can't believe I'm saying this," Deacon said, "but I agree with Artemis, Chelsea. Maybe we should just let this one go? We do have a wedding to focus on after all."

"Hey, I'm with you one hundred percent babe. As far I'm concerned, we are *done* with mystery business. From now on its vacation and wedding!"

"Ten bucks says she's back in an hour," Glenda muttered to Lizzy.

"You're on!" Lizzy muttered back.

I stood up from the table, rolling my eyes at my aunt and cousin. "Have my corner, for once?"

"And where are you going now?" Glenda asked. "Sneaking around to look for clues?"

"I'm going to the bathroom. Last time I checked that was still allowed!"

"She's got you there, Glenda," Lizzy said.

I walked away from the table, adding another eyeroll for good measure, and made my way over to the bathrooms on the other side of the patio. As I came around the corner, I saw a sign in front of the bathroom door. "Cleaning, open again in ten minutes."

I asked the nearest member of staff for directions to the next closest bathroom. "Follow the path around the back of that building," the young woman said. "There are more bathrooms around there."

I thanked the young woman and followed the path around the building. Halfway along the route I tripped over something and almost broke my neck. Looking back at the dimly lit path I saw coils of garden hose that were sticking out of the bushes. I cursed the lazy gardener that had left the hose there, pushed it off the path with my foot and continued to the bathroom, realizing the young woman had directed me to the bathrooms in the foyer.

After refreshing I made my way back into the foyer, deciding to walk back through the hotel to avoid any more hose-tripping incidents. I walked past the front desk and recognized Mable, the woman that I overheard getting fired on our first day.

"Ah, Miss Sponks!" she said. "I heard you were reunited with your luggage!"

"Yes. It's Mable, isn't it?" I asked. She nodded. "Forgive me for asking, but weren't you… let go?"

"Ah, yes," Mable said with an awkward nod. "Victor did fire me. The hotel board asked me to come back temporarily to help fill Victor's absence."

I noticed Mable's eyes were red and her cheeks blotchy, she'd clearly been crying. "How are you holding up?" I asked. "You worked for Victor for a long time, didn't you? The news must be hard."

"It's very hard," she said. "I hate to say I told him so but look what happened. I told the old man that woman would be the death of him. Lo and behold I leave and later that night he's dead! I'm just glad they finally arrested her."

"Yes well… the police will certainly take care of things!" I said, not wanting to dive back into the case again. "Good to see you again."

"And you," Mable said.

I started back in the direction of the restaurant when another familiar figure came around the corner. Sunny Saupo's eyes lit up in recognition. "Just the woman I was looking for!"

"I'm in the middle of dinner with my friends and family," I said, keen to avoid whatever this was.

"Fear not Sponks, it's all wrapped in a neat bow now! I thought you'd just like to see the killer bit of evidence that superstar Sheriff Saupo procured. Footage of Mrs. Roberts in the pharmacy!" Before I could even make the shape of the word 'no' with my mouth Sunny whipped out his phone and it started playing a video.

"Is this necessary?" I asked, recognizing the pharmacy from my visit the other day. The camera looked like it was above the desk, pointing down at the front door.

"Look at this!" Sunny said, ignoring the question. "In she walks, so brazen! Hood up, as if that obscures her face! But you can see it's her, clear as day!"

"I mean the footage is a little grainy, but yes, it looks like her."

January Roberts walked into the pharmacy wearing a hood and shades, the hood drawn over her head. She approached the counter and a moment later was walking away with a paper bag—inside which was the lethal prescription.

"Wait, this is the best part!" Sunny said excitedly. I watched patiently as the figure of January Roberts accidentally caught her head on one of the signs dangling down from the ceiling. I narrowed my eyes as I watched her leave the pharmacy. Sunny just burst out laughing. "Talk about a smooth criminal, eh, Sponks?!" he roared. "Anyway, just thought you'd want to see that. I'll let you get back to your meal now. Good night!"

Sunny walked away, singing and dancing—clearly in a very good mood. I couldn't help focusing on the curious part of the footage where January Roberts hit her head on one of the pharmacy's ceiling signs. I was halfway back to the patio area when I saw Koa—the staff member that had been loading January's bags into the van the night Victor died.

"Koa, right?" I asked him. He stopped and nodded.

"Yes, Miss Sponks, how may I help?"

"What time did you load Mrs. Roberts things into the van two nights ago?"

"It was eight, miss," Koa answered.

"You're sure?"

"Yes, it was right at the end of my shift, I remember because I just wanted to clock off."

"Where was she going?"

He shrugged. "I don't know. I just drove her to the dock. Somewhere on the mainland, that's all I know."

I thanked Koa and was about to head back to dinner when a niggling feeling made me pull out my phone. I dialed the number for the coroner's office. Jill answered.

"Hello?" she asked.

"Hi Jill, it's Chelsea Sponks. Are you working late?"

"I'm at home, the phone bounces to me out of hours. Everything okay, Chelsea Sponks?" Jill asked.

"I was just curious about time of death," I said. "Do you know what time Victor Roberts died?"

"Yes, I believe we put it somewhere around ten in the evening."

"And how long does it take for someone to die from a morphine overdose?"

"Oh, minutes," Jill answered. "If at all…" After a short pause she said, "Whatever is the matter? These questions lead me to believe you suspect something is awry."

"I think there might be a problem with our timeline," I said. "The prints suggest January Roberts was the one that gave the poisoned water to Victor Roberts—"

"That's right," Jill affirmed.

"But I have it on good authority that she left the island two hours before his time of death. It couldn't have been her."

There was another moment of silence before Jill answered. "The evidence seems overwhelmingly against her otherwise."

"That it does, but it doesn't quite add up. I think I might have to speak with the Sheriff about this."

"That's probably for the best," Jill said. "Let me know what comes up, Miss Sponks. For all we know Mrs. Roberts snuck back on to the island to kill her husband."

"That's a very good point, goodnight, Jill."

"Goodnight, Miss Sponks."

I put my phone back into my bag and made my way back to the dinner table, where Deacon, Lizzy, and Glenda were arguing about which Back to The Future film was the best.

"Uh-oh," Glenda said as I sat down at the table. "I know that look!"

"What look? I'm just sitting down!" I said in my own defense.

Lizzy and Deacon were smirking too. Deacon leaned in sympathetically. "It's your mystery face, something is wrong."

"My mystery face?" I said.

"Yeah, you kind of furrow your brow and pout your lips," he said.

"But you just said you're going back to vacation mode," Lizzy recounted. "So, it can't be a mystery. I mean, who could find themselves inspired to pick up a case just from going to the bathroom?"

"Listen… if the three of you could walk in my shoes for a minute. The universe *throws* this stuff at me." The three of them burst into laughter.

"What happened?" Deacon asked. I recounted my short trip to the bathroom and back again. After hearing my story, he softened. "Okay, that's actually quite unusual. From the sounds of things January Roberts can't have been the killer. She left the island before Victor died!"

"But all the other evidence suggests the contrary," I recapped. "Something else is bugging me too. On that surveillance footage she hits her head on one of the pharmacy's ceiling signs."

"Well, that happened to me," Deacon said. "Not that out of the ordinary."

"Right, except you're over six feet tall. January Roberts is shorter than I am, and I didn't hit my head on those signs!"

"Maybe she was wearing heels?" Lizzy asked.

"Maybe. I'd have to look at the footage again."

"One thing's for sure…" Glenda said slowly as she took a sip of her drink. "Chelsea ain't done with this one yet!"

"I am for tonight. I'll tell you that for free. Come on Deacon, let's go back to the room. I am done with today!"

After saying goodnight to Lizzy and Glenda, Deacon and I made our way back upstairs to the room, keen to put the day behind us.

"I'll tell you what I'm ready for," Deacon said. "A good bath."

I kicked my shoes off, getting ready to melt next to him in bed. "Sounds good, followed by a good night's sleep and a bit of rest."

I was about to make my way over to the bed when three quick knocks came at the door. Turning around I saw an envelope slide under the door and come to a stop on the carpet. I quickly went over to the door, pulled it open and looked both ways down the corridor to try and find the mysterious courier—the corridor was empty.

"Odd," I said, picking up the envelope and opening it.

"What is it?" Deacon asked, sitting up on the bed.

"Oh, just the usual, you know, people posting mysterious messages under the door and running away before I can catch them." Inside the envelope were two slips of paper. Upon the first there was a note.

'Miss Sponks, by now you've probably realized that all isn't as it seems in this case. I'm afraid you're the only one that can set things straight—this should tell you everything you need to know.'

TURNING the note over I found nothing else. I opened up the second piece of paper, which was folded up and written in a different ink and handwriting. The contents of this second note were much more confusing.

'EDRS – CA & OD: C17HNO.
Make it so, or you will be next.'

I HAD to read the second note several times over just to try and understand, but I found myself only drawing blanks. As with the other note, the reverse side of this one was blank. There was nothing else inside the envelope.

"What in the world?" I muttered to myself.

"Fan mail?" Deacon asked as he came over to me. I showed him both of the notes and he was equally as perplexed.

"What is it? Some sort of code?" he asked, squinting at the second note. C17HNO? What is that? A car registration perhaps?"

"That's not a bad idea," I said. The rest of it was completely foreign to me though."

Deacon shook his head and chuckled. "So much for you getting a good night's sleep," he said and laughed. "No chance you're falling asleep now."

"No…" I said as that irritating realization came over me. "I suppose not."

CHAPTER 12

The next morning my first visit was to Sunny Saupo, whom I found enjoying breakfast out on the patio before the other guests had woken. Sunny was reading a broadsheet Hawaiian newspaper, and he met me with a delighted grin.

"Ah good morning, Miss Sponks! Take a seat, take a seat! And what a delightful morning it is too! Beautiful, isn't it?! Did you sleep well? I myself, I slept like a baby, though I can't profess to understanding the saying, having had a few nippers myself I can tell you that babies sleep on their own terms!"

"You seem especially talkative this morning, sheriff," I said, taking a slice of toast from the table and pouring myself a glass of juice.

"I'm in good spirits, Sponks, aren't you? This mystery business with Roberts is behind us, and the only thing remaining now is the freight container. How did you get on with that yesterday, by the way?"

I paused for a moment, my mouth hanging open as I collected my thoughts. I'd come down here this morning to talk about the Roberts case, by all accounts it was *not* behind us. "Uh, the freight container… right." I scratched a hand through my head as I shifted gears. "To be honest Sunny nothing about the freight container case makes sense."

"Oh, ho?" Sunny said with an intrigued brow. "Please, share the details, Miss Sponks. Perhaps this is another case for Master Detective Sunny Saupo! I'll find the swine that took that container!"

"I already found him," I said. That got Sunny's attention and he turned his head.

"You did?"

"Yes, and he wasn't a swine, he's an old Japanese sailor named Hiroto."

Sunny nodded in recognition. "I know Hiroto, the old sea dog! Well, why didn't you tell me you found him? I'll send the men at once and have him arrested!"

"Because he was just doing his job. Hiroto showed me his manifest, picking up the container was a scheduled job, and get this, he said the container was empty and its doors were open."

"Impossible!" Sunny said defiantly. "I saw that container an hour before it vanished, and it was not empty!"

"Right, well, Hiroto claims it was. Furthermore, he gave me the address and contact details of the person that requested the job. We went to the address and found an old beachfront property that was taken out in a storm years ago."

"A burner address…" Sunny said in thought.

"It would appear so, but it doesn't stop there. We found a coffin that was nailed shut at the address, and inside that coffin was the phone number that was on Hiroto's manifest. Whoever asked him to pick up that empty container gave that fake address and nailed their burner phone inside a coffin too—they wanted us to find this."

Sunny looked at me like I'd grown an extra head, but there was also a giddy excitement about him, like he couldn't quite believe what he was hearing. "I must say this just gets better and better. What a confounding mystery this is. What do you make of it, Sponks?"

"I think I'm ready to wash my hands of it. Mysteries are often confusing, but they still usually make sense. Nothing about this makes sense."

"Nonsense, I think perhaps you just need to take a step back and things will become clearer. I will have the boys down at the station take a look at this address and number, see if we can't pull up any more information."

"Anyway, that's not why I came to speak to you this morning," I said, clawing my way back to the topic at hand.

"Oh?" Sunny said, lifting up his little cup and sipping his coffee. "What did you want to talk about?"

"It's the Roberts' case, specifically January's involvement."

"Did you want to watch the surveillance footage from the pharmacy again?" Sunny asked proudly, whipping his phone out to show me the clip again. "You know I dare say they'll give me some sort of award for this case, it's not every day one—"

"January Roberts didn't kill her husband," I said flatly. Sunny tripped over his own words, appearing confounded by my conclusion.

"But she had to! The evidence is all there! The fingerprints, the pharmacy footage, the morphine results from the autopsy!"

"Yeah, once you take all that into consideration it seems pretty damning, but there's another thing we've overlooked completely. The night Victor Roberts died I was taking a walk through the gardens, I overheard January Roberts shouting at one of the hotel staff as they packed her things onto a van. She left the island at eight, and Jill from the coroner's office said time of death was at ten."

Sunny blinked a few times as he processed the information. "Then she can't have left the island! There is no other option!"

"And I suppose we will examine that today, but there are other things that don't add up here, Sunny."

"Such as?"

"The pharmacy footage. On her way out of the pharmacy January hits her head on one of the ceilings signs. I've been in that pharmacy, and I didn't hit my head."

"So what?"

"So what? She's shorter than I am! How could she hit her head? Show me that footage again!" Sunny did playback the footage, though a little more reluctantly this time. When I brought up the discrepancy with Jill, she suggested maybe January Roberts was wearing heels, but no—there were no heels on her feet in this footage.

"Perhaps the sign has been lowered…" Sunny said thoughtfully as the clip finished.

"Or perhaps that isn't January Roberts," I said.

"But her face!"

"What about it? She has a hood up, and she's wearing shades. For all we know it's a mask."

Sunny laughed outrageously at this. "Miss Sponks, can you hear yourself? A mask? This is Diamond Island; we do not have sophisticated criminals like that!"

"It's either that or January Roberts' legs magically grew a foot taller." Which wasn't an option, even *with* magic considered.

"I'm sure there's a very simple explanation for all of this," Sunny said.

"There is, though you won't like it: January Roberts is innocent."

Still, he shook his head, his voice reducing to a shrill whisper. "I just can't see it."

"There's something else too," I said, pulling out the note that was pushed under my door last night.

"Mother Mary weeps!" Sunny said, the last of his good mood eroding under my barrage. "What now?!"

"This was pushed under my door last night, two notes." I handed the notes to Sunny, who opened and read them both. An intense look of examination came over his face. "Who gave you these?"

"I don't know, when I opened the door there was no one there. What do you think the notes mean? The second one specifically."

"*'EDRS – CA & OD: C17HNO. Make it so, or you will be next,'*" he said, reading the note out loud. He twisted his lips and looked up at me. "It's gobbledegook, no? I mean the second part is a threat of some sort, but the first part—Miss Sponks I think the answer here is very simple."

"You do?" I asked in surprise.

"Yes, someone is trying to throw you off the scent," he said and handed the note back to me. "I don't think it's important."

"Someone is sending me anonymous notes concerning the case, that's got to count for something. Deacon suggested maybe the latter part is a car registration. C17HNO. Could you run it for me?"

"I suppose I could," Sunny said, though I could tell he didn't like the idea. "Actually, no, that's a great idea Sponks. I'll run the registration and see what comes up."

"You think it's worth pursuing then? The note does mean something."

"Who is to say?" Sunny asked with a casual shrug. "You are the superstar sleuth however, and I'm inclined to follow your intuition."

"Brilliant, well we have a few things to do today then in that case. On the night of Victor's death January took a boat to the mainland. If we can get surveillance footage or eyewitness testimony placing her on that island it rules her out as a suspect, she couldn't have done it given the forensic timeline provided by Jill."

"I'll have my men look into it, but Miss Sponks let me raise another question, what if the forensic evidence is incorrect somehow? What if the time of death was earlier?"

"You'd swear by the evidence to condemn a woman, but doubt it when it doesn't fit your conclusion?" I surmised. "Sheriff, I think you're making that fatal mistake again with starting at the end and working backwards."

Sunny smiled, as though I'd caught him in a trap. "You know what Miss Sponks you are right once again; I keep making the mistake of letting the evidence carry me away."

"I want to speak with January Roberts," I said. "We need to find out why she went to the main island, further solidify her alibi." Just then something came to me. "You know what, sheriff, I think perhaps we've been going about this whole thing the wrong way regardless."

"How's that?" Sunny said, taking another sip of his coffee.

"We know the murderer staged the suicide, which means they wrote the suicide note."

"That is correct," Sunny said.

"The suicide note had the combination to the safe, which means the murderer knew what was inside the safe."

"…Also correct," Sunny agreed.

"So, if January Roberts was the murderer why would she have left the other two wills in the safe? If she knew the physical presence of the other two wills would nullify her will, then why leave them there?"

"An astute point!" Sunny said shrewdly. "But what does it mean?"

"I'm beginning to suspect that the three people named in the wills had nothing to do with this at all. Instead, I think the murderer was someone else altogether, and they left the three wills in the safe to divert attention. What happens to the estate if there is no legal will and testament?"

"But there are three!" Sunny countered.

"Three that contradict one another, which means none of them is valid," I recollected. "So, what happens to the estate?"

Sunny sputtered, like a schoolboy that had been caught sleeping at the back of class. "I must confess, I don't know."

"Then we need to get to the bottom of that as well. But first of all, I'd like to speak with January Roberts. Have your men see if she shows up on the surveillance footage for the dock on the mainland. In the meantime, we can talk with her this morning and figure some more things out."

Sunny sat forward and placed his head in his hands, I could tell his good morning had been thoroughly undone. "Sweet Mary Magdalene, this case isn't behind us at all, is it?"

"No sheriff, it isn't," I said. "Sorry, did I ruin your breakfast?"

An uncharacteristic frown came over the large sheriff and he stared into the distance, wistfully mourning the imagined accolades he'd been daydreaming over only minutes before I came along. He sighed sorrowfully and collected himself, a determined smile coming back over his features. "Ah, what is this but a small sidestep? We will get to the bottom of this Miss Sponks, that is for sure." Sunny finished the last of his coffee and stood up from the table. "Let's go and speak with Mrs. Roberts then and see what she has to say. I have a feeling this is going to be a long day!"

CHAPTER 13

It was arranged that I would go over to the station to see January shortly. Before that I decided to head back upstairs to see Victor Roberts' room and investigate the crime scene once more. As of yet the only lead I really had in this case now was the mysterious note that had been pushed under my door, and its mysterious contents whereas of yet unknown to me.

The elevator doors opened on the top floor of the hotel and Sunny's men, who were still playing cards at a table next to the elevator, met me with a familiar nod. I nodded back and walked down the corridor to the room, opening the door and weaving through the crime scene tape zig-zagged across the frame.

It was quiet inside the room, and uncomfortably still. I walked over to Victor's bedroom, turned on the light and waited in the doorway a moment to let myself survey the scene. The walls and ceiling were still brushed with this slight darkness, that I still couldn't explain. One of the maids said the walls and ceiling had not been like this before Victor died, so what could it mean?

I headed over to the windows on the left-hand side of the room, at the moment they were both closed. I opened them both to let the room air out a little, taking a moment to look more closely at the strip of paint missing from the interior of the window on the right. When I first came to the crime scene this window on the left was open.

The window provided a nice view of the hotel grounds, and the palm tree forest that ascended over the mountainous part of the middle island. Down below there was a path that hugged the perimeter of the building, followed by a luscious green lawn that ran for thirty feet before meeting the trees. Looking down I realized the path was the same one I had walked on last night to use the bathroom in the foyer. It was the same path I'd tripped over on some discarded hose and nearly broke my neck.

Ducking back inside I looked at the rest of the room and found nothing of interest. There was no secret compartment in the safe, no items lost under the bed or cabinets. The only mystery in here remained the darkened walls and the paint missing from the window —and also the tacky air conditioning vent over the bedroom door.

Back downstairs I met one of Sunny's men in the foyer. Sunny had arranged for one of his men to take me to the station where January Roberts was currently being held.

"Ready to go, Miss Sponks?" the officer said with a friendly smile.

"Lead the way," I responded.

Fifteen minutes later we arrived at the police station in Diamond Island village. The officer led me into Sunny Saupo's office, where Sunny and January Roberts were sitting across from one another at a large desk. January was cuffed and wearing an orange boiler suit.

"Ah, here she is!" Sunny said with relief, standing from the chair and gesturing for me to take his place. January Roberts did not turn to regard me. "I'll leave you alone a moment while I speak with Kev, I think we've got a lead on that dock footage."

"Very good," I said. "The sooner the better."

Sunny slipped out of the room, and I sat down across from January. Her face didn't betray any sort of emotion, other than mild annoyance. "I thought you were supposed to be some sort of world-famous super sleuth?" she said dryly.

"I'd consider myself more a c-list curtain twitcher," I joked.

"Keep cracking jokes," January responded. "I guess it's all fun and games for you, meanwhile an innocent woman is locked up for a crime she didn't commit."

"For what it's worth I know you're innocent," I said.

A look of shock came over January. "Then why did you lock me up? This *is* some sort of set up! Wait until my lawyer hears about this!"

"Relax," I said, holding my hands in the air to ease the situation. "Your arrest had nothing to do with me. After the police got their hands on the surveillance footage, they thought they had a home run, I think they got carried away with themselves. I'm helping out here, but Sunny still has the final say in things."

"I don't know how they did it, but the person in that footage is not me," January said. "You have to believe me."

"I know it's not you, and Sunny doubts so too. The person in that footage hits their head on one of the pharmacy's ceiling signs, you're much too small for that. I know, I've been in that pharmacy myself, and I'm taller than you—I didn't hit those signs."

"So, it *is* faked!" January said in astonishment. "Call my lawyer, I want out of here immediately!"

"Relax, there's still the other evidence condemning you. Can we talk about that?"

"What other evidence?"

"The fingerprints mainly. They were on the box of pills and the glass of water that contained the fatal dose of morphine. The entire scene suggests you gave Victor the water—his prints weren't on the glass. Your prints were on the letter too."

January's mouth opened and closed. "I don't know how to explain any of that. I didn't give Victor his drinks, he was old, but he wasn't an invalid. I was his wife, not his nurse!"

"I'm just reiterating why you're still in hot water."

"But the pharmacy footage was faked! They stole my face somehow! Doesn't it stand to reason then that they stole my prints too!"

This time I was the one that faltered. "Well, I—uh, I suppose that hadn't crossed my mind."

"It should!" January said, keen to have caught me off my guard. I must admit I hadn't considered this line of thought at all. "It seems simple when you think about it! Though… I don't know exactly what it means."

"I think I might be starting to get an idea," I said. "Let me ask you something, the walls and the ceiling in that bedroom are slightly darkened, as though effected by mold. The maid says they weren't like that before Victor died, can you confirm that statement?"

"Yes, I can," January said. "I don't know what happened to the walls or the ceiling."

"What about the window frame?" I asked. "There is paint missing from the inside."

January turned her head. "I don't know what you're talking about."

"Chipped paint on the frame, the window was damaged somehow. Was it like that before?"

"No," she said and shook her head, her eyes narrowing in confusion. "You think that has something to do with his death?"

"I don't know at the moment, but clearly there are unknowns that we haven't yet accounted for. I must say the evidence gives you one favourable advantage," I said.

"It does?" January asked in keen interest. "What's that?"

"Time of death. The coroner put Victor's time of death at ten in the evening, but I know for a fact that you were off the island by that time. You were packing your bags into a van at eight, and you took a boat to the mainland. As of yet you've been reluctant to provide an alibi. If you could help us understand where you were, it would go a long way to clearing your name."

"I was on the mainland, I don't think *why* matters, does it?" she said guardedly.

"In any normal situation we're entitled to our privacy, but this is a murder investigation Mrs. Roberts, any information you provide could help to clear your name."

January stared at me silently for a moment before responding. "I was on the mainland, that's all you need to know—there's no further detail required than that."

Just then a knock came at the door and Sunny Saupo came back into his office with one of his men. "Okay Roberts, you're free to go," he said glumly.

January looked as surprised as me. "What happened?" I asked. Sunny pointed his thumb at his accompanying female officer, who provided the answer.

"Footage on the mainland dock shows Mrs. January Roberts disembarking at nine in the evening, and we have eyewitness reports that she was seen in *La Palma* restaurant, attending dinner with a gentleman around ten. She wasn't on Diamond Island when Victor Roberts died."

"Eyewitness reports?" I asked. "How did you find them so readily?"

"Oh Mrs. Roberts is quite famous around the island," the female officer said keenly. "You are a local celebrity, are you not, Mrs. Roberts? All the gossip magazines love her."

I looked at January, who let out an incensed breath and pursed her lips. "Get me out of these handcuffs then, I want out of here now."

"Who was the gentleman?" I asked. "The one you were having dinner with?"

"Just a friend, what does it matter? The evidence proves I wasn't on the island, so I couldn't have been the one that killed Victor." Sunny nodded for his accompanying officer to uncuff January Roberts, who then stood up and brushed her fingers through her hair. "Take me to my things. I want to get out of this place immediately— you will be hearing from my lawyer."

With that January and the officer walked out of the room. Sunny looked at me and shrugged.

"What do we do now?" he asked, scratching his head. "We've lost our only suspect, and so reluctant to explain her alibi."

"Yes, though given the circumstances I think I have worked out why."

"Oh?" Sunny said with an intrigued look.

"Isn't it obvious?" I asked. "She was clearly cheating on Victor Roberts with this other man, and I bet my bottom dollar the couple have a prenup between them. Adultery is a surefire way to get yourself written out of an estate."

"Ah…" Sunny said, drawing the word out long and quietly. "That does make sense! But the three wills nullify themselves anyway. Surely she knows she gets nothing!"

"Perhaps she's holding out for hope regardless," I sighed. "Anyway, we need to examine all of the evidence again," I said. "The pharmacy footage is clearly faked, and I'm starting to suspect the fingerprint evidence has to be faked too."

A grave expression came over Sunny. "By the way I ran the registration from that note you received, it's a minivan in Maine."

"Something tells me it's not a minivan in Maine," I noted, seeing as we were thousands of miles away. The letters and numbers had to mean something else then.

"Oh, one positive note, I have that address and phone number—the coastal shack and the phone inside that coffin—I had the boys search, and both the address and phone are registered to a *Mrs. Enid Ma*—Chinese name perhaps? We have quite a few Chinese out here now. She's registered at an address on the Koli Tolo islands, it's a three-hour boat-ride from here, if you like I could arrange for us to go there tomorrow—"

"No," I said, waving one hand in his direction while I pressed the fingers of my other hand against my forehead. "Don't bother, it's another waste of time."

"Waste of time, whatever do you mean, Miss Sponks?"

"I don't know what's going on with this freight container business exactly, but the whole thing feels like it's been set up as one giant time sink. Don't you see it, *Mrs. Enid Ma?* Mrs. *Enigma*—it's a spoof name, a deliberate fake."

Sunny stared at me blankly for a second and then his eyes lit up in recognition. "Ah, Mrs. Enigma, I get it now! How wildly clever!"

"Yes," I said with complete disinterest. "A real head-scratcher. Now if you don't mind Sunny, I think I'm going to go back to the hotel and get back to the vacation for a bit while I can. I trust your men can take care of this enigma business. As for the Roberts case I really cannot find any course of investigation at the moment."

"So, you're giving up?" Sunny asked.

"Not giving up, I'm just stepping away from things. I find sometimes when I hit a dead end that the best thing to do is step away and give myself some distance. Once I come back, I will have a fresh perspective on things."

"Bravo!" Sunny said. "A great idea. I think giving yourself some time to think can only strengthen our position, when you come back, I'm sure we'll be ready to but this business behind us!"

"Somehow I doubt that," I muttered.

CHAPTER 14

"It sounds like this January Roberts really is innocent then," Lizzy remarked as we ate dinner together on the hotel patio. Artemis was in his astral form lazing on the wall next to us, Glenda had booked herself in for a 'Mega Deluxe Palm Tree Massage' in the spa, and Deacon was back in the bedroom on a video call with his parents—who were due to arrive at the hotel tomorrow.

"Remember Chelsea, it's always the one you least suspect," Artemis said, ever so helpfully.

"So, it's one of the astronauts off the international space station?" I asked sarcastically.

"Or the ghost of Dean Martin!" Lizzy said, joining in with the heckling.

"If I could blow a raspberry I would right now," Artemis said, throwing in a scowl for good measure. "I'll just say the word 'raspberry' and leave it there. Raspberry."

In response Lizzy stuck her tongue out and blew an actually raspberry at him. A passing waiter looked at her in confusion, as only Lizzy and I could see Artemis in this magical form—making Lizzy look a little bonkers.

Artemis snickered as he saw Lizzy blush. "Mwah ha! That's instant karma for you there, Lizzy!" Lizzy pressed the stone on the amulet, hoovering Artemis back into the magical item.

"There, that's better, isn't it?" she said cheerfully. I rolled my eyes and laughed.

"What have you been up to today anyway?" I asked her. "Hiding in your room from the sun again?"

"Nah, I actually ventured outside today. Glenda and I went jet skiing. I set up an invisible magical forcefield to act as a sun barrier. This china doll skin can't be in the sun for longer than five minutes, even with SPF 50—I go cherry tomato red almost straightaway. Oh—before I forget, Gloria wants you to go over some things with me before she gets here."

"Where is she anyway?" I asked. "For a wedding planner she is curiously absent, considering the big event is in a few days."

"I have no idea, but she's definitely sorting things behind the scenes. She's left a bunch of binders behind the front desk; we have some things to go through together. I don't know if you want to sort through some stuff now while Deacon and Glenda are busy."

"Sure," I said. "Sounds like a date. Let's go, amigo."

I followed Lizzy to the reception, where we were greeted by Mabel. She looked a little better than she did the other day, her eyes and face less blotchy from the crying. "Hello Sponks party," Mabel said genially. "Did you want those books, Lizzy?"

"I did, you read my mind."

Mabel smiled and pulled a large plastic box from under the counter, inside which were three thick white binders. "What are these?" I asked.

"A basic itinerary of the day—or so Gloria informed me," Lizzy said. "We have a few things to go through and pick."

"A few?" I said in a disbelieving tone. Looking at the size of those binders we'd have to set aside a few hours at least. "I thought she was sorting everything!"

Lizzy laughed. "She's sorted most of it, I think she just wants to let you put your own personal touch on a few things. There are parts for Deacon to help with too—it's just as much his day of course."

"Alright," I said, already feeling a little flustered. "Let's cart this stuff upstairs then and we can—"

Just then all the lights in the hotel turned off, plunging the foyer in the darkness. "Ah, buggery heck—agh!" Mabel said from behind the desk. I heard a loud clatter as she tripped over something and crashed to the floor.

"Are you okay?" Lizzy asked.

"I'm fine, just tripping over," she said. Under my breath I muttered a quick incantation to help me see in the dark. I didn't have crystal clear vision, but it was better than facing the pitch black. I saw Mabel push herself back up again, her eyes wide and searching as she tried to navigate the darkness. "I don't suppose either of you have a phone, or a torch?"

"Back in our rooms," I said. "We're trying to do the whole screen free thing, you know, being present in the moment of a vacation."

"Is there something we can help with?" Lizzy asked.

"The main generators have tripped, they're in the basement. Tana usually takes care of it, but he must have fallen asleep."

"Tana?" I asked.

"Yeah, he takes care of all the stuff down in the basement, if only I had a torch."

"Listen I've got pretty good night vision," I said. "Do you want me to go and speak with him?"

"Are you sure? It's so dark in here, I can't see a thing," Mabel remarked.

Without my incantation things would be pitch black, but as it stood, I could see pretty well, like standing in a dimly lit room. "What can I say, I ate a lot of carrots as a kid. Lizzy, can come and help me too."

"Just as long as you let me know where you got those carrots…" Lizzy said. She was hinting that she didn't know how to do the night vision spell but couldn't communicate that in front of Mabel.

"Where's the basement?" I asked Mabel.

"The first right after the elevators, there's a door—but you'll need a key. I saw Mabel turn around blindly in the darkness and pat her hands against the wall, trying to find the key for the basement. The wall with the keys was actually to her right. I moved behind the counter to help her.

"On your right," I said. "Which key is it?"

"It's on the bottom right, the word 'basement' is written on the tag."

I found the key straightaway. "Got it! Alright Lizzy, let's go!"

Mabel stared into the darkness in amazement. "You can really see in this light?"

"What can I say? Those carrots man…"

I headed back around the counter, took Lizzy by the hand and led her to the basement door. Once we were out of earshot of Mabel, Lizzy piped up.

"Okay, how did you do this night vision spell?" she asked.

"Repeat this three times and hold your hands over your eyes: *Black eyed shark, white snow stark, take the shadow and the dark*," I said. Lizzy did as I said, and I saw her eyes glow purple with the faint light of magic—invisible to mortals.

"Where do you learn these spells?" she asked in amazement. "You've got a spell for everything, and you've barely been a witch for a year."

"I read a lot of books," I said with a shrug. "Come on, let's go and turn these generators back on."

We unlocked the basement door and headed down a set of stairs. I'd be lying if I said it wasn't a little spooky. The stairs opened into a large underground boiler room, it looked like the kind of place a killer and teenagers would have their final showdown in an eighty's slasher flick.

"Well, this is straight out of a horror film," Lizzy muttered.

"Ha, I was just thinking that!"

"Hello?" a voice called from the dim room. "Is anyone there?"

Lizzy and I both stilled and looked at one another. We were on a metal walkway which overlooked the room. Down there in the darkness I saw a young man standing next to a bed in the corner.

"Who's that?" I called out.

"My name is Tana, I work down here. Who's that?"

"I'm Chelsea Sponks, I'm a guest here at the hotel. I'm here with my cousin, Lizzy as well. We came to see why the power went out."

"The generator just cuts out some time," Tana said. "I would have fixed it by now, but I fell asleep sorry, my bad. Do you have a light source? I can't find my torch anywhere?"

"I can see it from here, hold on a second."

Lizzy and I headed down the stairs and walked across the basement to the corner where Tana had his makeshift sleep area. I handed him the torch from the table. "Thanks," he said, turning it off. The bright light burned against the pitch black, I silently dispelled my night vision spell and saw Lizzy do the same.

"How did you do that?" Tana asked. "It's pitch black in here."

"I've always had good night vision," I lied, adding a shrug for good measure. "How do we get this generator back on then?"

"It's the big unit over there," Tana said, pointing at a metallic brick about the size of a minivan. "Let's have a look and see."

Tana was a young man, probably in his early twenties. He was large, Samoan, and had the same genial nature that many of the islanders had. His voice carried a friendly warmth. "The breaker probably just tripped, that happens every now and then, but then—" Tana paused as he came round to a panel of electronic switches. "Nope, it's not the breaker. Huh."

"That doesn't sound promising," I said.

"I'm not an engineer or anything," Tana said, "So I can troubleshoot a few basic problems. Nine times out of the ten I just have to reset the breaker, if it's not that then we might have to get someone into look at this thing. I'll have to unlock the main panel and—huh," Tana paused again.

"What is it now?" Lizzy asked.

"It's the maintenance panel, it's usually locked, see?" Tana pointed at a metal flap that protected the generator's interior control unit. He lifted the flap up, exposing the generator dashboard.

"Where's the key?" I asked.

"Over in a box on the wall over there. I never leave this thing unlocked, it's not safe." Tana headed over to a metallic key box on the wall and opened it. Inside were a dozen hooks with keys, but one hook was empty. Tana looked at me with an uncertain expression. "The key for the generator is missing. It also unlocks the windows too."

"Windows?" we both asked. Tana pointed across the room to a row of narrow slit windows that were near the ceiling.

"Outside those windows are on the ground level, though they're behind some bushes on a path behind the hotel," he explained.

"I think I know that path," I said. "I nearly broke my neck on a hose that was sticking out of the bushes."

"Who has access to these keys?" Lizzy queried.

"Just me. I last used them a week ago. I have to do a quick diagnostic of the generator once a week." Tana went back to the generator and completed his walk around. As he reached the last side, he jumped to attention upon seeing a tube had detached from the side of the generator. "You're kidding me! How did this come undone?!" Tana quickly picked up what looked to be some sort of extraction tube and clipped it back into the side of the generator. He looked at us and mopped his brow. "Boy, that was a close one!"

"What was a close one?" I asked, none the clearer as to what had happened.

"I don't know how much you know about generators, but we almost just died."

"Let's assume we both know next to nothing," Lizzy said to him.

"Because we don't," I clarified. "What happened?"

"Generators like this pump out carbon monoxide. That tube I just plugged back in, it extracts the deadly carbon monoxide fumes to a vent outside, where they harmlessly vent into the atmosphere. In a condensed space like this they could suffocate someone in a few minutes. I know why the generator shut off now, it's carbon monoxide alarms must have tripped."

Looking up at the ceiling I noticed it was brushed with some sort of black, just like the walls and ceiling in Victor Roberts' room. "What is that? Mold?" I asked Tana as I pointed at the dark marks on the ceiling.

"Soot residue from carbon monoxide," Tana said. "Look, follow me." Tana walked back around to the generator's dashboard, pointed at a small light in the top right and nodded. "Yep, see? The generator will switch off if it detects a leak like that. Ooh, boy! That was a close one!" he repeated, not seeming overly concerned that he had nearly just died.

"Is it normal for an incredibly important tube like that to just come out?" Lizzy asked with uncertainty. I noted when Tana had put the tube back in four clips fastened around the seal to help hold it in the place.

"No, not at all. I don't even know why it was undone in the first place. Somebody must have been tampering with this thing. That would explain why the keys are missing as well."

"Might be worth mentioning this to Sunny," Lizzy said to me. "If someone is messing around with dangerous equipment like this people could get hurt."

"I can tell him," Tana volunteered. "I'll see him later anyway at the family barbeque."

"You're related?" I asked.

"He's my uncle," Tana clarified. "We're having a celebration for the Diamond Island Wildlife Charity. This Roberts business has all been pretty terrible, but it's good news for them."

"Why's that?" I asked, turning my head.

"You know with the estate going to the charity and all. Apparently, there was a bunch of conflicting wills or something? In Hawaiian law if that happens an estate passes to a charitable organization—voted on by island council. They picked the Diamond Island Wildlife Charity, good money to a great cause!"

"Wow," I blinked. "Well… at least the money isn't going to waste."

"Yeah, and Victor Roberts himself was a frequent donator to the charity, so you know the money is going to a good place. Anyway, thanks for helping out with the generator. I owe you one! Let me help you out. Y'all have a good night now!"

CHAPTER 15

The next morning, I found myself on the beach at the front of the hotel. Deacon and I had gone for an early morning swim and spent the rest of the morning reading in the shade. The rest of the guests were going to start arriving at the hotel today for the wedding and I was sure the real bedlam was about to start, so I wanted to enjoy the island's relative quiet while I still could.

"I'm going to head back to the room and shower before lunch," Deacon said after finishing his book. "You want to come?"

"Nah I'm going to soak up some more sun and try and finish a few more chapters of my book. I'll meet you at the table at the usual time?" With a parting kiss Deacon made his way back to the hotel, leaving me alone to enjoy the sea, the sun, and the sand.

After about twenty minutes I put my book down and rifled through my handbag to pull out the notes that had been pushed under our hotel door the other day. I still had no idea what the mysterious code meant, and I was no closer to understanding either.

'EDRS – CA & OD: C17HNO.
Make it so, or you will be next.'

"WHAT ON EARTH DOES IT MEAN?" I muttered to myself having read it now for the hundredth time. Suddenly I noticed a shadow pass over the sand and turning around I saw one of Sunny's officers behind me. It was a young Hawaiian woman, the badge on her lapel said 'Verity'.

"Ah, good morning, Miss Sponks!" she said warmly. "Sunny asked me to try and find you. He said he's sending some men out to see 'Miss Enigma' today, if you wanted to accompany? He said you would know what that means."

"I do, and I'm good. Tell him no, but thank you."

"I most certainly will," she said, smiling cordially. "What do you have there, a bit of light reading?" she said, nodding to the note.

"Oh, just a note that was pushed under my door a few nights ago," I said. I handed it to her, not really thinking much more of it. Verity took the note.

"Electronic Death Registry Service – Cardiac Arrest and Over-dose… Make it so, or you will be next," she read. I practically jumped out of my beach recliner, standing so fast that the young officer jumped back in startlement. "Miss Sponks is everything okay?!" she said in alarm.

"You know what that note says?" I gasped in amazement.

"…Yes," Verity said, her brow creasing with amused confusion. "Should I not?"

"Read it again," I said, circling around to stand next to her as she did so. "How did you know the code?"

"Code?" Verity asked. "It's not code, just shorthand. Very common shorthand as well. EDRS stands for Electronic Death Registry Service."

"What is that?" I asked.

"It's a database, an official ledger. When someone dies, they are added to it, along with information like cause of death, time of death —the usual stuff. After that it says—CA & OD, which stands for cardiac arrest and overdose."

I gawped. "What about the letters? The vehicle registration?"

"Registration?" she asked in confusion. "No, it's probably some sort of chemical formula, though I don't know what. I'm not a chemist. Where did you get this note again? It's very unusual," she said.

"Pushed under my door..." I said absently, connecting the dots in my head. The person that pushed this under my door had left another note, stating that 'things weren't as they seemed' and that this note would bring things to light. I looked at Verity. "How come you can read this?"

"I deal with this sort of thing on a weekly basis. All Hawaiian police read shorthand like this, when we deal with a coroner or insurance companies. I work on the mainland mostly, there's a lot more activity over there, let me tell you."

"I showed this note to Sunny, he didn't know what it meant."

Verity looked confused more so. "I find that doubtful, although Sunny has always had an aversion to technology, perhaps he never bothered to learn the shorthand—I don't find it likely though. He would almost certainly know what this means."

"Yet he didn't..."

"Of course, there is a simpler explanation," Verity said calmly.

"That being?"

"The big buffoon probably didn't have his reading glasses on!" she laughed. "He's very vain, never wears his glasses, but he needs them alright. Don't tell him I told you."

"I think I know what this chemical formula means, but I want to make sure. Verity... thank you, thank you! You have been amazing!" At once I gathered my things and started running back to the hotel.

"I'll tell Sunny it's a no on the Enigma business then?" Verity called after me.

I FOUND Doctor Herman Klaus in the hotel bar, he was sitting with a fancy looking cocktail, reading over some very dry paperwork. On my approach he turned and smiled at me in delight.

"Ah, you finally reconsidered that offer for a drink then?" he asked.

"First of all, you're like thirty years older than me. Second of all, shut up." I pulled up a chair and sat down next to the irritating doctor, fishing the note out of my pocket as I did so. I pushed it across the bar to him. "What does this say?"

Doctor Herman Klaus adjusted his reading glasses, squinting at the handwritten note. "I don't know, a bunch of random letters?"

"The part at the end," I urged. "The part that looks like a registration, is it a chemical formula?"

He looked at the note again and read it out loud slowly and uncertainly. "EDRS—CA & OD. CH17HNO… ah. Morphine."

"Morphine?" I said quickly.

"Yes, it looks like morphine. The chemical formula is ah…" he paused, holding his fingers against the bridge of his nose while willing an answer from his memory. "C17 H19 NO3. Yup, that's morphine."

"But the letters on this note don't exactly match."

"Correct, probably a lazy lab tech or something. You're lucky you got numbers at all to be honest. A lot of those techs would just write CHN and be done with it. That's the problem with this generation of 'scientists', absolutely no work ethic, no determination, no attention to detail and—"

"Just shut up a second will you," I said, putting a hand in his face to quiet him as I tried to think. With Herman's deduction I could now decipher the note fully. I took the note back off him and read it out loud to myself.

"Electronic Death Registry Service – Cardiac Arrest & Overdose: Morphine. Make it so, or you will be next."

"Ah, EDRS—" Herman said, snapping his fingers as though he was annoyed he hadn't guessed it. "I should have got that—though I don't work with that side of things much, more the research for me. What's the note about Sponks?" he asked, taking a sip of his drink.

"If I was to make an educated guess, I'd say someone threatened the coroner."

"The coroner?!" Herman said in surprise. "Whatever for?"

"To obfuscate the crime scene, and make it look like something it wasn't. What if Victor Roberts didn't die of a morphine overdose at all, what if it was something else altogether."

"You know it's funny you should say that," Herman said. "The crime scene hasn't set well with me at all, and I've not been able to put my finger on why until now."

"Go on?" I prompted.

"Well, I realize now it's the symptoms. They're *close*, but not entirely in line with what I would expect from a morphine overdose. The tell-tale signs were missing—blue lips and blue fingertips."

"These are commonly expected symptoms of a morphine overdose?" I asked, my mind already racing.

"Oh yes, the fact that Victor had neither is actually very unusual. To the point that I would say that—"

"He didn't die of a morphine overdose at all—he died from something else."

"Yes!" Herman said, almost delighted that I had read his mind. "Which—"

"Calls into question the forensic evidence surrounding this case, because it all seems to be—"

"Wrong!" Herman piped, keen to finish the sentence.

"Forged was my word of choice, but yes…" I stood up from the bar, my next destination fixed firmly in my mind. "Don't talk of this to anyone. I don't know who I can trust now."

"Even me?" he asked, taking another sip of his drunk.

"Unfortunately, you seem to be mostly harmless, even if you are downright irritating. Keep your lips sealed, your life may depend on it."

"Mom's the word," Herman said, pretending to zip his lips shut. Without wasting another second, I ran back to the elevators to return to my room. I had to find Deacon, I needed someone to accompany me on the next part of this mystery. I was getting close to the killer now, and I couldn't do this alone.

* * *

Diamond Island Coroner's office wasn't what I had in mind. It was a small building that looked like it had been built back in the seventies. The front door opened into a shoebox room that acted as a sleepy reception. I rang the bell on the counter and looked around the office, studying the framed degrees and newspaper articles upon the walls.

"This whole building feels dead," Deacon muttered beside me.

"You're telling me," I said back.

A door behind the counter opened and I saw a lanky young man poke his head out, I recognized him vaguely from the crime scene a few nights ago, he was Jill's assistant. "You came!" he squeaked.

"Uh, yes," I said. "Randall, was it?"

"Roger," he corrected, his voice breaking as he did so. "I was starting to think you weren't going to show up."

"You were… expecting me?" I asked.

"Yes! I didn't know who else to turn to, seeing as how—well, you know by now. It's not safe to talk about, but I don't really know who else we can turn to. Jill wouldn't ask for help, she's just as terrified, heck, probably more so—"

"Slow your roll, junior," Deacon said calmly. "What's going on here?"

"You came here about the note, right?" Roger asked.

"You're the one that pushed the note under my door?" I asked.

Roger nodded nervously. "I had to say something, this sort of thing has never happened before!"

"What sort of thing?" Deacon asked.

"Being threatened to fake forensic evidence," I said. "Where's Jill?"

"She's in the back," Roger said. "Follow me!"

We followed the lanky young man into the back, where we saw a rather stressed-out looking Jill sat at a computer. "Oh, for heaven's sake, can't you just go away?" she asked upon seeing us.

"Good morning to you too," I said. "You look a little strung out, Jill, what's going on?"

The coroner tapped her fingernails against the desk, pushed her hands through her hair and took a deep breath. "Nothing is going on, everything is fine."

"Everything isn't fine," Deacon said. "Someone threatened you with a note, they made you forge forensic evidence. Why?"

"I… I really can't talk about it," Jill said. "Please just go."

"Was there any morphine in the water?" I asked. "Was January Roberts' prints even on the glass? Who made you forge the evidence? Is your life at risk?"

Jill stood up from the desk, she looked like a woman that was living on the edge. "You have to go, now. Just get off this island and don't look back. It's not safe."

"You have to tell us who's doing this," Deacon repeated.

The terrified woman just shook her head silently. "I can't. He threatened my family."

"He?" I asked.

"Please go, now," she said. "If they know you're here… just go!"

Deacon and I looked at one another silently and left the coroner's office without another word. "So, someone is threatening her," he surmised. "But we're no closer to learning the truth."

"On the contrary I think the truth is right in front of our faces. I think I know who the killer is."

"You do, who?" Deacon asked.

"Let me hold onto that for a moment," I said. "I want to check out the local art gallery first."

"The local art gallery?" he said, scoffing in disbelief. "Are you joking? Come on Chelsea, we're closing in on the killer here!"

"I know, but this is part of it, I promise. Look, it's only down the block." I pointed at the building at the end of the street. The look on Deacon's face told me he thought it was a waste of time, but he agreed anyway.

"Alright, let's go then."

We reached the closed art gallery a moment later, the blinds on its windows pulled shut, and the door locked. No one else was around at the moment, it was just Deacon and I out on the street.

"Okay, the gallery is closed. Now what?"

"Now we use magic to break inside," I said.

"What?!" Deacon remarked.

"Eh, don't get your knickers in a twist. You knew who you were marrying."

I placed my hand on the doorhandle and muttered an unlocking incantation under my breath. The lock clicked and the door popped open, revealing a large and spacious room in which there were half a dozen cellophane-wrapped pallets with large objects upon them. We stepped inside and closed the door behind us.

"What's this?" Deacon asked as I approached one of the large objects. I grabbed a boxcutter from a table near the door, went over to the nearest pallet and slashed open the opaque white plastic wrap. It split open, and inside there was a large ceramic bull.

"This Deacon is *art*. More specifically it's the half-dozen ceramic bull sculptures that supposedly went missing from the beach a few days ago."

"But Sunny said they were stolen!" Deacon said in confusion.

"Yes, and resultingly we've been running around these islands on a wild goose chase, wasting our time, when all along the sculptures had never been stolen—they were exactly where they were supposed to be."

"Nothing on this island makes sense," Deacon said.

"No, it's all starting to make a lot of sense. Up until now nothing has made sense because it was all done by design. I understand it all now though, let's go to the police station."

We walked back to the car and drove to the police station. Inside I met Verity behind the desk. "Ah, hello again, Miss Sponks! Fancy seeing you again today."

"Where's Sunny?" I asked. "I found his missing bulls."

"He's just at his house, getting ready for a big family barbeque tonight. They're celebrating of course—his wife's charity has been voted as the recipient of the Roberts estate, quite the haul!"

I looked at Deacon, my mouth dropping open in amazement. "It's his wife's charity. The money's going to her!"

"Wait a minute—" Deacon said. "You mean to tell me—"

Just then the door to the police station flew open with a crash and there I saw a red-faced Sunny Saupo standing, wide-eyed and out of breath. "Verity, arrest them both at once! It was them! They're the ones that killed Victor Roberts!"

"I uh… what?" Verity asked with a note of confusion.

"Never mind, I'll do it myself!" Sunny barked, pulling the gun from his holster. "Get on the ground now, both of you, I'm arresting you for the murder—"

"Of Victor Roberts?" I asked. "The crime that you committed?"

"Verity, you saw that! She reached for a gun! I'll have to shoot to kill!" Sunny said as he raised his own gun up, placing the sights on me —who very much did *not* have a gun. With my eyes focused on the gun I channeled all of my magical energy on heating up the metal, the gun turned white hot in a second and Sunny dropped the burning gun to the ground, screaming as he looked at his blistered hands. "My hands, my hands are on fire!"

Without missing a beat Deacon stepped forward and swung his fist into the rogue sheriff's jaw, Sunny Saupo stumbled back and smashed through the glass doors of Diamond Island Police Station, hitting the path outside with a heavy thud as he rolled around and groaned in pain.

"What on earth just happened?" Verity stuttered from behind the reception desk.

"We just apprehended a murderer," I said. "Call in the rest of the station. This mystery is over."

CHAPTER 16

"Get me out of here this instant!" Sunny Saupo roared from his cell. The police station was now a hive of activity, every active officer on Diamond Island having come back to the station in the last half hour. There were even officers from the mainland too. One of those officers, a short woman with dark black hair, came into the room with a stern look upon her face. At her arrival everyone fell silent, even Sunny.

"Okay, somebody care to tell me what this madness is all about?" the short stout woman announced in a clipped voice.

"Sheriff Kahale, you have to let me out, this is one big understanding! You need to arrest that woman!" Sunny proclaimed from behind the bars of his cell.

The sharp-eyed woman turned her gaze on me and lifted an enquiring brow. "And you are?" she asked me.

"Chelsea Sponks," I answered. "I'm here to get married, this is my fiancé, Deacon Long."

Sheriff Kahale nodded astutely. "I see. My name is Kaili Kahale, I'm the head sheriff preceding over all of Hawaii. I was on a boat with some of my men when a signal came in there had been an attack in Diamond Island Police Station." She looked about the crowd, her eyes settling on Verity this time, Sunny's second in command. "What's going on here, Verity?"

"It's to do with the Victor Roberts murder, Mrs. Kahale," Verity said respectfully. "This here Chelsea is a sleuth of sorts, she was helping Sunny get to the bottom of things. About half an hour ago Miss Sponks here came to heads with Sunny, she says he was the murderer."

Sheriff Kahale looked at Sunny. "Is this true, Saupo?" she asked calmly, her hands clasped behind her back.

"She's the murderer, Sheriff Kahale! Her and that fiancé of hers!" Sunny said, his eyes wide and black with humane desperation. "Get me out of this cage at once!" Sheriff Kahale shot Sunny a look at this order, and he swallowed and changed his tone to be more respectful. "Uh... *please*, Sheriff Kahale."

The short woman looked around the rest of the room. The small police station was full to the brim now with officers, about thirty men and women in total. Sheriff Kahale twisted her mouth and looked at Verity. "I'm guessing you have Sunny Saupo locked up for a good reason," Sheriff Kahale hazarded.

Verity nodded. "Yes miss, his behavior has been a little unusual. Miss Sponks and her fiancé came into the station, and Sunny burst through the doors a few minutes later, all red in the face and out of breath. He pulled a gun out and said he was going to shoot to kill, he said Miss Sponks had drawn a weapon on him—but she hadn't."

"Lies!" Sunny shouted. "Lies! She tried to kill me, Sheriff Kahale, they both did, they're the—"

"Silence!" Sheriff Kahale shouted. Sunny fell silent immediately. "Okay, let's take this from the top, shall we? I have places to be, and not a lot of time to waste. Miss Sponks, it's my understanding you were working as an amateur investigator of sorts, in line with Sunny Saupo and his department?"

"Yes," I said. "That's correct."

"Very well, then tell me why this man is behind bars, and tell me as quickly as you can. I have a goat curry waiting for me at home, and it's getting cold."

"It began several days ago, when Victor Roberts was found dead in his personal suite back at the White Diamond hotel."

"Found dead by her no less, the real murderer!" Sunny shouted.

"Mr. Saupo if I hear one more word from you, I will put you in the gallows myself," Sheriff Kahale warned. "Sit down and shut up!" Sunny did in fact sit down on the bed in the cell, though he didn't look happy about it. "Continue Miss Sponks."

"From the offset it looked like Victor Roberts had killed himself, a deliberate morphine overdose," I said. "But from the get-go I could tell some things about the crime scene didn't make sense."

"Such as?" Sheriff Kahale asked.

"The walls and ceiling were slightly darkened, as though effected by mold. One of the windows was open, and paint was missing from part of the frame. In addition to this the air conditioning vent above the door was tacky."

"Meaning?" the sheriff asked.

"I'll get to that in a moment, if you'll allow." She nodded her head. "Victor Roberts was found with a suicide note in his hand, along with the code to the safe in his room. Inside this safe we found three wills, leaving the estate to three different people. The wills contradicted one another, and therefore each of them was void. At the time I didn't know what would happen to the estate, and Sunny Saupo claimed he didn't know either."

Sheriff Kahale turned her head in confusion. "Why, the estate would be donated to a local charity, voted by a council of elders. Sunny Saupo, you know that—every Hawaiian police officer worth their salt knows that!"

Sunny said nothing, so I continued. "Yet he proclaimed he didn't know, when I asked him. After that we talked with the three people named in the will, Victor's wife, his son, and an old friend that helped him start the business many years ago. Each was a suspect at first, but very soon January Roberts emerged as the leading suspect."

"Why?" Sheriff Kahale asked.

"Evidence," I answered. "The evidence showed that Victor Roberts died of a morphine overdose. A glass of water next to his bed contained fatal amounts of morphine. There was an empty box of prescription painkiller boxes in the bedside trashcan—the active ingredient was morphine—those pills were taken out in January Roberts name. Her prints were on the box and the glass of water, Victor's weren't, suggesting she gave him the water, and mixed the pills into the drink."

"I see," Sheriff Kahale said. "Anything else?"

"Footage from the island pharmacy, showing Mrs. Roberts picking up the prescription of pills—though the footage aroused my suspicion almost instantly, Mrs. Roberts is short of stature, and the person in the footage hits their head on a ceiling sign in the pharmacy, a sign than I didn't touch with my own head, and I am taller than Mrs. Roberts."

"So, the footage was faked," Sheriff Kahale surmised. "But how?"

"My guess would be a mask of sorts, though we have not found one yet."

"I see. So, despite this the evidence until this point almost over-whelmingly suggests our culprit is Mrs. Roberts. Where is she?"

"She was freed recently," I said. "Established time of death told us that Victor Roberts died at ten in the evening. January Roberts left the island that night at eight, two hours before he was supposed to die. A morphine overdose would be almost instant, so she couldn't have been the one that killed him. Surveillance footage and eyewitness accounts confirmed that January Roberts was on the Hawaiian main-land at the time her husband died—it couldn't have been her."

"So, the evidence must be incorrect in some way," Sheriff Kahale said. "But how?"

"The answer actually came to me in a note a few days before, though I didn't understand its contents at the time. I pulled the note from my handbag and handed it to Sheriff Kahale, who read it imme-diately without issue.

"Electronic death registry service, cardiac arrest and overdose..." she paused at reaching the chemical formula for morphine and I prompted her. "Morphine... make it so, or you will be next." Sheriff Kahale looked up at me. "So, someone threatened the coroner."

"Yes," I said, "though the note mystified me for several days. I showed it to Sunny Saupo on the first day I received the note, and he said he did not understand its contents."

Sheriff Kahale rolled her eyes once again and looked at Sunny Saupo. "Saupo, what is this nonsense! Any police officer could read this shorthand!"

At this point Deacon piped up. "Um, excuse me?"

"Yes?" Sheriff Kahale said to Deacon.

"I'm a police officer, and I didn't know what the note meant."

"Oh?" Kahale said with a raised brow. "Do law enforcement officials not deal with this type of shorthand back in America?"

Deacon shook his head. "No, no we don't. We have a different system altogether apparently."

"Well, the system we have here is very commonplace, and every Hawaiian police officer knows this shorthand, including you, Sunny Saupo! I should know, I taught it to you myself!" Sunny remained sitting in his cell, his jaw clenching in silence. "Feigning ignorance of estate procedure, and legal shorthand! How ludicrous for you to obstruct justice like this!"

"As soon as I realized Sunny was lying to me, I think I knew he had something to do with this, but I still didn't understand why, or how. The answer started to come to me when there was a power cut back at the hotel—I went down to the basement with my cousin to find Tana, a young man that attends to the generator."

"Yes, I know Tana, Sunny's nephew. What did you find down there?"

"Several more clues," I said. "A tube that vents carbon monoxide had come loose, that was why the generator shut off. In addition to that a set of keys were missing from the basement, keys that open slit windows to the grounds outside. The ceiling of the basement was brushed black with some strange substance, just like the walls and ceiling in Victor Roberts' room. Tana said it was soot residue from the carbon monoxide. Tana himself was the one that gave me the killer clue—he said he was going to a barbeque this evening, to celebrate a local charity receiving the Roberts estate. That charity, as it turns out, is run by Sunny Saupo's wife."

Sheriff Kahale rolled her mouth again, looking more annoyed with each revelation. "I think I've heard enough. I've been in this game long enough to figure it out now." She looked at Sunny. "You killed Roberts, tampered with his legal documents so the estate would go to a local charity—one owned by your wife of course! What do you have to say for yourself!"

"You can't prove anything!" Sunny shouted. "I want my lawyer! I'll sue this station for every last penny! You have no evidence!"

"On the contrary I think the evidence won't be hard to find," I said.

"Oh?" Sheriff Kahale asked me. "What makes you say that?"

"Deep down something tells me Sunny Saupo is very proud of this crime. To his credit it was extremely sophisticated, though he had to strong arm a lot of people to cover up the real truth. I think he is arrogant enough to have held the key evidence, I wouldn't be surprised if he has it locked away somewhere secure, either his home or his office."

"I'll check his desk!" Verity said. "There's a locked drawer. We can break it open!" Verity rushed off at once. Sheriff Kahale looked at me again.

"So, it wasn't morphine. And you're saying the forensic evidence was all forged?"

"Yes, I believe the coroner and her assistant were threatened by Sunny. One of the officers was supposed to be bringing them here." As if on cue Jill and her young assistant, Roger, came into the station, both looking overly concerned.

"Is it true, Madame Coroner?" Sheriff Kahale asked Jill. "Did this man threaten your lives? Do not worry now, you are safe."

Jill nodded shortly, and I realized she was shaking from nerves. "Y-Yes," she stammered. "He said the evidence had to bury January Roberts. It was all faked, the prints, the morphine in the water and the system, all fake, all of it."

"And the mask," Roger piped up. The attention turned on him.

"Mask?" Sheriff Kahale asked.

"Sheriff Saupo demanded pharmacy footage of the wife collecting the pills. I had to make a mask based of her likeness, it wasn't great, but I pulled it off. The pharmacist doesn't have the best eyesight."

"But the camera doesn't miss a trick," I said, looking at the tall and gangly assistant. "You hit your head on the ceiling sign."

"Yes," Roger stated. "It was difficult to see in that thing. He said he'd kill us if we didn't do what he said! We didn't want anything to do with this!"

"So how did Victor Roberts actually die?" Sheriff Kahale asked. "I'm assuming you must have taken a real autopsy, even if Saupo had you fake the results."

Jill opened her mouth to answer, but before she could I jumped in. "Suffocation," I said. "From carbon monoxide."

"That's correct!" Jill said in shock. "But how could you know?!"

"Putting together the missing pieces," I said. "A few nights ago while having dinner at the restaurant I followed a path around the building to find the bathrooms in the foyer. On the way there I nearly tripped and broke my neck on a hose that had been left in the bushes. At the time I assumed it was a negligent gardener, but after visiting the basement I realized the truth."

"You'll have to spell this one out for us, Sponks," Sheriff Kahale said.

"That path was directly underneath Victor Roberts' bedroom, and the wall behind the bushes contains the slit windows from the basement. The cable that vents carbon monoxide came loose because Sunny Saupo disconnected it several nights prior and ran a hose up the side of the building, through the window of Victor Roberts' room. He used tape to create a seal around the gap in the window, and the air conditioning vent above the door. Victor Roberts suffocated to death without knowing he was being poisoned. Then Sunny came in, removed the evidence and planted the suicide note."

"Heresy!" Sunny shouted from his cell. "Lies, all lies! Sheriff Kahale you must realize it is *her* that is the murderer, I am innocent, I—"

"Found the motherload!" Verity said with a big smile as she came back into the room. "This was in his locked desk drawer!" Verity was holding a duffel bag. She held it upside down, tipping its contents onto the station floor. There was a mask of January Roberts' face, a roll of duct tape, a crumpled-up ball of tape with flakes of white paint stuck on the inside, the missing set of keys from the basement, a keycard to Victor Roberts' room, plastic gloves, two blister packs of unopened morphine pills, a notepad and a box for a cellphone.

Sheriff Kahale leafed through the notepad, shaking her head as she read through its contents. "Saupo, you absolute fool, you diarized everything!"

At this point Saupo finally broke. "Well, I would have gotten away with it, if it wasn't for her!" Saupo shouted, pointing a finger at me. "It was genius, genius! And let's face it, the money is better in the hands of the natives than in the hands of that greedy old bastard!"

"Sheriff Saupo!" Verity said in disgrace.

"I should have seen it from the beginning," I said. "Sunny was behind it all along. He even came up with a plan to distract me, knowing that I would be on the island. He claimed a freight container of valuable art vanished into thin air. Thus followed a bizarre clue hunt, one that was designed to keep us away from the hotel and waste our time."

"She's right," Sheriff Kahale said. "Saupo wrote about it here in his journal! He set up a clue hunt that would have them running in circles, when in fact the art was delivered all along!"

"Which I confirmed myself an hour ago when I broke into the art gallery," I admitted. "The sculptures have been there all this time. Saupo even arranged for our luggage to be switched with a delivery of frozen fish, another distraction to waste our time and inconvenience us."

Kahale looked at Saupo as though he was mad. I expected him to start roaring his lies again, but to my surprise he just burst out laughing.

"Well, you can't deny that I made it interesting, eh Sponks?!" Saupo said, his words wrapped up in mad laughter. "I've certainly given you a vacation to remember!"

I said nothing to Saupo, but I turned my attention to Sheriff Kahale. "Was there anything else you needed to hear?"

"No," the demure officer said with a shake of her head. "I think you've explained everything, Sponks, even in the face of Saupo's deliberate red herrings. Bravo, your reputation truly does proceed you. Tell me this, where do you go from here?"

"Well, if you don't mind, I'd like to go back to the hotel with my fiancé. We're getting married tomorrow, and we've barely had a minute to figure out what's going on."

Sheriff Kahale laughed. "Very well. Right. Everybody, let's start cleaning up the mess that Saupo has left behind." She looked into the cell at Sunny. "I'm disappointed in you Saupo, you've let us all down."

Sunny just shrugged, sitting back down on the bed as he accepted defeat. "At least I made it interesting," he said. "Beats another day in mindless paradise!"

Collectively I felt everyone in the room silently disapprove of the mad sheriff, Deacon and I made our way outside of the station, where a squadron car was waiting to take us back to the hotel. Almost as soon as I sat down my phone started ringing. Looking at the screen I saw it was Gloria, our wedding planner. "Heads up," I said to Deacon. "Madness resumes. Hello?" I said as I answered the phone.

"Aloha darling where are you? We have a dress rehearsal in three hours!"

"We're coming back to the hotel now," I said. "We just had a little business to take care of."

"Chelsea darling, need I remind you that you're here to get married? I must say we have no more time for distractions!" Gloria bemoaned.

"Don't worry, Gloria, I have a feeling the distractions are behind us now. We're ready to focus on the main event," I said, smiling at Deacon and holding his hand on the back seat of the cruiser.

With Saupo behind bars and all the loose ends tied up, there was only one thing left to do—get married to the love of my life.

CHAPTER 17

"I now pronounce you man and wife!" the celebrant announced heartily from the altar. Deacon came forward and kissed me, and a triumphant cheer swept through the crowd of our friends and family.

It was a beautiful day on Diamond Island, the sun was high in the sky and the azure waters were lapping the white sand beaches. As we finished our kiss we parted, held hands and turned to the crowd to offer a comedic bow. Applause erupted through the air, with church bells ringing faintly in the distance.

A ukulele orchestra began to play, the soft music floating over the crowd as Deacon and I made our way back down the aisle towards the hotel. I saw various members of my family in tears, including Glenda, who was bawling louder than anyone. Mom and Dad were a little more composed, and my brother Rudy smiled and nodded in acknowledgment as I walked passed him. My Aunt Tasha and Uncle Hugh were present too—they must have shut Pendle Island Zoo for the weekend.

I saw Adam, my lumberjack friend and gardener, and his girlfriend Serena, a former houseguest of mine who was a good friend, but also a nightmare guest. Viktor Oblonsky, the large Russian wizard whom I had helped to control a wild area of time magic at the center of Pendle Island. There were even a few unexpected faces, Adina Lopez, the podcast queen whom I had made friends with recently, Belladonna Brewdock, the matriarch of our former rival witch family—she now had human legs again.

In fact, as we walked down the aisle, I realized just how many people from Pendle Island were here. Amongst them were close friends and family, but throughout the crowd were also the faces of people that I had helped in one way or another, during my time of solving mysteries on the island. I didn't realize just how many people Gloria had flown out here, and as we reached the back of the audience I saw Gloria, the woman that had helped plan all of this.

"There are so many people here," I said to her in amazement.

"Yes, I think Pendle Island's population is currently at a record low," she said. "A lot of people responded to the advert."

"What advert?" Deacon asked.

"I thought about making a conventional guest list," Gloria said, "but then I decided for a couple as well liked as you the best course of action was just to put an advert in the paper, welcoming anyone to the wedding of Deacon Long and Chelsea Sponks, if their lives have been touched by you in anyway."

At that moment I began to feel myself well up, a knot formed in my throat, and it felt tight. "Well, that's an emotional bomb to drop on a pregnant woman," I said, wiping a tear from my eye. "I didn't spend an hour in makeup this morning just to cry it all off!"

Gloria laughed. "I'm sure we can... *magic* it up again. The photographer wants to do a couple of the cliché shots now, and then we can get to celebrating properly, food, drink, music, all of that, you know the deal," she said, turning her hand through the air as though speaking on rote. I supposed she'd done this type of thing several hundred times.

"That sounds great," Deacon said. "Though we might have to sneak a sandwich in at some point."

"A tactical sandwich is awaiting your beloved wife in the horse and carriage, rest assured," Gloria said with a knowing smile. "Fear not, I'll take care of your stresses for the rest of the day. There's no problem that I can't overcome!"

I returned a thankful smile. Deacon and I were about to start walking forward to the horse and carriage when I noticed that the sand underneath my feet was wet.

"Hold on," I said, "The sand is all wet, I've stepped right in something."

"Which swine spilled their drink?!" Gloria said with accommodating laughter. "Celebrating too hard already!" She came in closer and lowered her voice. "Don't worry Chelsea, I've got a spare pair of dry shoes for you waiting in the car. Gloria accounts for everything."

It was then that I realized this wasn't a spilled drink, I froze on the spot, and from the look on my face Deacon could tell that something was wrong.

"Chelsea, what is it?" he asked.

"It's not a spilled drink. Deacon, I know what's happened," I said, my eyes wide with unexpected panic.

"What?" he asked.

"Whatever it is, we can handle it!" Gloria said graciously.

"My uh... my water just broke," I revealed quietly. Deacon and Gloria both went pale.

Gloria chuckled nervously, swallowed, and took a deep breath. "Worry not Chelsea, it's just a little hiccup, nothing I can't handle!"

The wedding planner offered a fixed smile for a few seconds, and then she started swaying.

"Uh, Gloria, are you alright?" Deacon asked.

"Fine, I'm fine!" she said through her smile, her eyes dilating and staring into some unknown distance. Her knees buckled and she fainted, collapsing on the sparkling white sand.

CLICK HERE to read the final book, Book 12: The Witch Must Go On.

THANKS FOR READING

Thanks for reading, I hope you enjoyed the book.

It would really help me out if you could leave an honest review with your thoughts and rating on Amazon.

Every bit of feedback helps!

~ **Ongoing** ~

Hallow Haven Witch Mysteries

Wicked Witches of Pendle Island

An English Enchantment

Compass Cove Cozy Mysteries

~ **Completed** ~

Wicked Witches of Pendle Island

Wildes Witches Mysteries

Raven Bay Mysteries

Wicked Witches of Vanish Valley

MAILING LIST

Want to be notified when I release my latest book? Join my mailing list. It's for new releases only. No spam:

Click here to join!

I'll also send you a free 120,000 word book as a thank you for signing up.

marawebbauthor.com

amazon.com/-/e/B081X754NL
facebook.com/marawebbauthor
twitter.com/marawebbauthor
bookbub.com/authors/mara-webb